Lucy Crawford

The History of the White Mountains

from the first settlement of upper Coos and Pequaket

Lucy Crawford

The History of the White Mountains
from the first settlement of upper Coos and Pequaket

ISBN/EAN: 9783337288402

Printed in Europe, USA, Canada, Australia, Japan

Cover: Foto ©Andreas Hilbeck / pixelio.de

More available books at **www.hansebooks.com**

THE HISTORY

OF THE

WHITE MOUNTAINS,

FROM THE

FIRST SETTLEMENT

OF

UPPER COOS AND PEQUAKET.

By Lucy, Wife of Ethan Allen Crawford, Esq.

FIRST PUBLISHED IN 1845.

WITH PREFACE BY HENRY WHEELOCK RIPLEY.

———

PORTLAND, MAINE:
HOYT, FOGG & DONHAM,
1883.

Printed and Stereotyped by B. THURSTON & CO.,
97½ Exchange St., Portland, Me.

.

CONTENTS.

PREFACE.

In reproducing the early History of the White Mountains, their discovery and settlement, written by Mrs. Ethan Allen Crawford, we are delightfully carried back to the days of our boyhood, when we first visited those grand old Cathedrals and Temples of Nature,—to the days of that freedom of thought and life so full of sunshine and hope, which followed our young footsteps among the many changing scenes of grandeur then undiscovered among those "Everlasting Hills,"—days, in truth, full of "romance and reality," when the world seemed but the great ideal and central unfolding in one mighty volume, the wonderful gifts and glories of the great Creator's hands. The History of the White Mountains at this period forms one of the most interesting subjects of modern times, and thousands have read, who have never visited them, that most charmingly descriptive and interesting volume, written and published in 1859, by that patriot Christian scholar and statesman, the Rev. Thomas Starr King. It was the writer's highest privilege to be a companion of Mr. King for several seasons among the mountains, and whether exploring among cliffs and crags, or midst the wildwood passes, or following stream by stream with rod and line, 'twas all the same, his great heart and soul was the embodiment of *nature;* living he breathed it, and dying has left its fragrance on the desert air. We can but *hope* that this *best of all* White Mountain histories may ere long be republished, to more extensively perpetuate his memory among the scenes he loved so dearly.

The present volume, which we present to the public, was written in the old stage days of John Smith, the Knight of the Whip, who for nearly forty years drove his elegant Concord coach from Conway to Portland, and who is now living, a hale and hearty bachelor, nearly eighty-five years old, at his adopted home, Fryeburg,—in the days of Abbott, Thom & Co.'s line of stages from Center Harbor to Conway, and through the White Mountains,—in the days, in short, when occurred those events of history, that, like the "Crawford," the "Rosebrooks," the "Willey" families, belong alone to the past. We shall endeavor, in our next edition, to give a general history of the early settlements of the towns comprising the Upper Coos, Gorham, Lancaster, Littleton, Colebrook, Whitefield, Bethlehem, Conway, Bartlett and Jackson in New Hampshire; also of the early settlement of the towns comprising the Pequaket country, and the writer's native town of Fryeburg,

Maine. We shall also give the history of the building of the Boston, Concord and Montreal railroad into the mountains, the Portland and Ogdensburg through the Crawford Notch, the Mount Washington Turnpike from the Glen House on the east side, to the summit, and the Mount Washington railroad from Marshfield on the west side to the summit, together with whatever events have occurred which will interest the tourist to the White Mountains since the edition was published in 1846.

In this edition we give a very perfect likeness of Abel Crawford, "the Patriarch of the Hills," copied by Conant of this city, from the original portrait by Chester Harding in 1846, and now in the possession of Mrs. Abby Davis Bemis, his granddaughter, of Melrose Highlands, to whom the writer is greatly indebted for the loan of it for present use. The likeness is strikingly correct, and will be recognized by many who nearly one-half century ago saw the original work in the parlor of the old Crawford House. "Old Crawford" was the first man who ever rode a horse up Mount Washington in 1840, then seventy-five years of age. He died in 1852, aged eighty-five years, and the little mound just this side of Bemis' station marks his last resting-place, while grand old Mount Crawford is his fitting monument.

I feel sure that the pleasure-seeking and beauty-loving travelers of this generation, as cosily seated in one of the triumphs of modern civilization, an observation car, they glide comfortably over steel rails far up the sides of the mighty mountains, will be glad to hearken to the echo of a voice from the misty past, a voice telling the story of these grand and magnificent scenes, telling it not in fine, modern phrase, but in olden, homely, quaint speech, yet full of rugged strength and earnest meaning, like the character of the pioneers of the mountains, like the mountains themselves.

It was my original intention to have added to Mrs. Crawford's history a modern history of the White Mountains, but owing to the failure on the part of various representatives of vicinities to supply me with the necessary data, I am unable to do so in this edition.

A knowledge gained by a close acquaintance of forty-five years with the mountains and their visitors, of the lively interest and enthusiasm felt for everything relating to the White Mountain region, leads me to confidently expect the necessity of the next edition shortly, in which the modern history will be supplied.

"If thou art worn and hard beset
With sorrows that thou wouldst forget,
If thou wouldst read a lesson that will keep
Thy heart from fainting and thy soul from sleep,
Go to the woods and hills; no tears
Dim the sweet look that nature wears."

H. W. RIPLEY.

INTRODUCTION.

EDITION OF 1845.

I<small>T</small> may be inquired by some persons, what has become of Crawford, the mountaineer, or Ethan of the hills. It will be the endeavor of the authoress of this tale to relate some of his misfortunes and adventures, briefly as possible, it being always a rule with him to make short stories and not go a great way round to effect a small thing.

This she has done, in his own language, as nearly as she could, for the information of others and the benefit of all of her own family whom she is desirous of bringing up and making useful members of society. These are all true statements of things which have taken place within her own knowledge, since she has been living with him. These facts he was unwilling at first to have published, as he did not wish to expose those who seemed to be against him. They have been stated in as moderate terms as possible, as we do not wish to injure the feelings even of enemies if we have any such. It will readily be seen why he was always involved in debt, if this history is read with candor and viewed in a right manner, as it

7

will show his misfortunes to have originated, first, in the fire, which left him a large sum in debt; next, in being obliged to build almost every year, so far from common privileges; and then, in the two freshets, which caused him a heavy loss of property. Taking all these things into consideration, it may be wondered how he succeeded in getting along as well as he did, under so many losses and disappointments. But, saith the poet :—

> "Pigmies placed on alps, are pigmies still;
> And pyramids are pyramids in vales."

And, as the scriptures saith of men of ancient times :—

> "There were giants in those days."

HISTORY OF THE WHITE MOUNTAINS.

CHAPTER I.

THE ROSEBROOKS.

HANNAH HANES was born in Brimfield, Mass., August 3, 1744, and at an early age she experienced religion, at the age of seventeen, I think she told me; and this religion supported her through many trying scenes of life; neither did it forsake her in the time of death.

Eleazer Rosebrook was born in Grafton, Mass., 1747; was married to Hannah Hanes, in March, 1772, and there they lived until after the birth of their first child, a daughter; and when this child was one year and a half old, he, like many other enterprising men, took his wife and child and came into what was then called Upper Coos (pronounced Quos), as far as Lancaster. Here they made a temporary stay, while he could look about and find a place to settle, until after the birth of their second child, a daughter. They then moved into the woods, up the Connecticut river, as far as Monadnue or Monadnock, now incorporated as Colebrook, nearly thirty miles from any inhabitant, and without a road. They took the river, in some places, for a guide; and in other places, they followed by marks of spotted trees, which were spotted for the purpose of shortening the distance,

1*   9

and then went into a little log cabin which had been previously prepared by Mr. Rosebrook, my grandfather.

Now, in the woods, making a beginning, setting an example for others to follow, suffering many hardships, and enduring many privations common to beginners in a new country, they did the best they could and tried to be content with their situation. They had provided themselves with a cow, the only favored domestic animal they possessed, and, having no pasture, or fence, she was at liberty to range about and go wherever she pleased. Many times did Mrs. Rosebrook, my grandmother, in the absence of her husband, shut her dear child up in her cabin and taking her infant in her arms, proceed into the woods in search of her cow, which she would be directed to find by the sound of her bell. Sometimes she was under the necessity of wading the river to get where the animal was, and then she would return home and find the deserted child safe, and, with the infant still in her arms, and followed by the other child, did she milk her cow. What courage must this woman have possessed, after being for many years among near relatives, such as parents, brothers, sisters and a numerous circle of friends and neighbors, who were near and dear to her, and changing them for the woods! What a contrast between having a large society and now being confined entirely to these her lisping children! What woman in these days could do this and not complain of its being hard or severe? But she had made up her mind to be content and industrious in whatsoever situation she should be placed, and having a monitor within, which would say to her that although separated from earthly friends, yet she had one that would "stick closer than a brother," and while filled with these thoughts, her fears of wild beasts, and many other things, would flee from her.

Their living was principally upon animal food; as God always provides suitably for every one who depends upon him and will apply himself industriously to obtain.

The woods were beautiful, and well stored with game, such as moose, deer, bears, etc., and hunters might, in a short time, kill and procure a sufficient quantity of this kind of food to supply their families a long time. Some of the flesh they would dry, and some they would smoke; and, in various ways, did they preserve it and make good wholesome food of it.

One grand article wanted now was salt, which was scarce and hard to be got, and they could not well live without it, in this fresh and mountainous country. Some families suffered considerably, by their children having their necks swollen; the disorder was attributed to the want of salt, which was afterward remedied, in a measure, by carrying them to the salt water, and giving them a plenty of salt fish to eat, and applying the skin of the salt fish to their necks; but they never wholly outgrew this trouble. I have heard my grandfather say, that while living in Monadnock, at one time he went on foot to Haverhill, and bought one bushel of salt, and carried it home, through the woods, on his back, a distance, at that time, as they followed the river the most of the way, of not less than eighty miles. Can this same country produce a man now, with such wonderful power of muscle and strength of mind, to endure this and not complain of its being hard? But such was the courage of these hardy new beginners that they did not mind trifles. One circumstance I think worth recording.

One Major Whitcomb, who lived in this country, went on foot to what was then called Lower Coos, a distance of fifty miles from where he lived, and it was late in the spring; as the people had planted, in that place, he had great difficulty in finding potatoes, which it was his whole business to obtain; but he at length succeeded in getting one bushel of small ones, and these he carefully carried home, on his back. Those which would answer to cut, he cut in pieces, and then planted them. Afterward he counted the hills, and there were four hundred hills of these planted potatoes; and, in the fall, he harvested them, and had one hundred bushels of good potatoes. Such was the plentiful increase of almost everything put into the ground. So much so, that this country was considered by people, two or three hundred miles distant, to be equal to the western country now; and those who left their friends to come to this Upper Coos, (as they then termed it), were generally a robust and self-denying people; and the friends whom they left behind thought much more of the distance, than we do now of going two or three thousand miles; and their expectations of seeing them again were much less than now; which may well be imagined, when we reflect that it is more practicable to travel ten miles now, than it was to travel one then.

About this time was the revolutionary war between the United States and Great Britain. Grandfather volunteered his services, as he possessed the same independent spirit as our forefathers, and was determined as they were, to free our country or shed his own blood in its defence. Before he started, fearing for the safety of his family should he leave them alone, lest they might be destroyed by the enemy, he removed them down to Northumberland, and placed them in a sort of fort, which was then erected and guarded by the husbandmen; they then embraced each other, and he took his leave of his family, having a firm belief that if he had entered rightly into a good cause, he should be prospered, and impressed with these feelings they separated, while his wife's prayers were constantly for him and the general good of the country. But here, in this situation, she did not remain long, having then the addition of another child, a son. A gentleman by the name of White, kindly gave her an asylum in his house. As his wife was sickly, and not able to work, he gave her and her three children their board for what they could do; which she considered a great kindness, as it gave her the privilege of supporting herself and family without being chargeable to her husband.

Mrs. Rosebrook remained where she was, on permission, until her husband came home. He then moved his family to Guildhall, Vermont, and having settled them there, returned to his duty for a number of months, discharging it with bravery, and encountering his foes, whenever he was called upon, like a brave soldier.

He and an officer were once sent to Canada as spies. They were suspected, and finding it out, they made good their retreat; they were closely pursued by the enemy. Grandfather was aware of it, and they traveled night as well as day, until they came to a considerable stream of water; here they built a fire, and then put it out, to make it appear as though they had been gone for some time; they then waded the stream, and, when at a proper distance, struck up another fire and dried and rested themselves. The enemy came soon after, and found where they had made the fire, which they had extinguished, and, supposing they were out of their reach, returned; as one of the pursuing party told him afterward; and he likewise said, that he told them it was useless to follow further, as Mr. Rosebrook was a hunter and a woodsman, and knew better than to suffer himself to be overtaken.

Grandmother, while living in Guildhall, in the absence of her husband, was frequently visited by the Indians. As she was a woman, and alone, they seemed to make her habitation their place of resort, there being no man to resist them. By disposing of their furs, they would provide themselves with a plenty of what they called uncupy, or spirit, which they carried in bladders, taken from moose, and, at times, they would have a great drunk. This troubled her much, knowing their savage dispositions; she, fearing she would offend them and incur their displeasure, bore with them; at one time, however, she became decided and cleared her house of them, all but one, and she was so far gone under the influence of the spirit, or liquor, that she lay motionless upon the floor; grandmother took her by the hair of her head, and with the strength of her feelings, dragged her out of doors; and the squaw by being put in motion, came to herself so much that she had the use of her limbs; she drew her tomahawk and aimed it at grandmother, who had just closed the door after her, when this tomahawk came so near as to take off the wooden thumb-piece from the door handle; thus she providentially made her escape. Some time in the night, the squaw so far recovered as to move herself out of sight of the house; and the next day, after getting sober and recollecting how ridiculously she had appeared, and what trouble she had caused the good woman the evening before, came back and freely asked her forgiveness, and likewise said she would not do the like again; and she strictly kept her word.

Grandfather came home again, on permission, and as his wife had so much trouble with the natives, and her family being again increased, she did not well know how to have him return; and as he had enlisted during the war, he hired a man to take his place, and remained at home to assist his helpmate in bringing up her young family. As they had begun to fulfil the commandment which was given to Adam, at the beginning, it became necessary she should have help; and as a reward for his toils and hardships during his services, he was paid off in old Continental money, which proved a nuisance to him. I have now some of it still in my possession, which I keep in remembrance of his courage and valor.

Peace was proclaimed, and they remained in Guildhall, and the people were, for a number of miles, seemingly all of one family, sharing in each other's bounties and enjoying one another's company, like so many brothers, and if one happened to get a dainty, or a rare nice thing, an invitation would immediately be given to the neighbors, who would assemble, and they all would have a social time of it. There was no distinction in those days in point of dress or grandeur, but all wore their own manufacture. I have heard my grandmother say that when she was dressed in her striped, short, loose gown, and her clean starched and well ironed blue and white checkered linen apron, she felt much better then to appear in a meeting, among christians, than she has since, when dressed in silks. They then, had no ruffles, no ribbons, or anything that appeared like ostentation, but all was neat and tidy; as this was the uniform manner of dress in those days, they all enjoyed it without a murmur and felt happy. The men wore garments made of the skins of moose, which they had learned to dress of the Indians; they were, as they said, cold things to put on in the morning, but when once warmed, the cold weather could not penetrate through, and they would last a long time. For shoes, they made of this same kind of skin, a substitute called moccasins, until the country began to be opened a little, and then they got sheep; the wool, the women would card and spin; and such were their habits of industry, as this was a slow way to get their wool worked up, I have heard grandmother say that she used frequently to work a whole week, both night and day, without undressing herself. She would only lie down for a short time with her clothes on, while carding and spinning; when this was done she would weave it, and then with the bark of some forest tree they would give it a color; without the process of a clothier, or the workmanship of a tailor, they would cut their own garments and make them; and in this cheap, humble, but happy way, these people lived for many years, until the

enemy of contentment began to introduce articles of merchandise, which soon created pride, and a sort of rival-
ship commenced, and as soon as one came in possession
of a newly imported dress, it stimulated others to follow
the fashion, and one extreme generally follows another.
In this way has our country since been infested with this
foolish pride of dress, making gay the outside; while
some, it is feared, have neglected the most important
part, the soul; but another era, it is hoped, will take
place, which will yet cause all who watch for it, to be
more and more happy.

Now, while living at that time in this country, the
greatest disadvantage, which they felt most seriously, was
the want of good schools for their children. As they
seldom had any schools so near as to have the privilege
of sending them at all, their eldest went but one day,
their second, one week, which completed their school education. But, as their mother had in early life acquired a
knowledge of letters, and the proper use of them, she
instructed them so well that they could read and spell
with considerable accuracy. This they found to be useful
in after years, as they could read for themselves and
sometimes for others. For instance; the husband of the
eldest became afflicted with weakness of his eyes, so that
he could not himself see to read, and being drawn up
with the rheumatism so much that he could not walk, it
has been a matter of great consolation to him in his dull
hours, to sit still and hear her read; and thus time passed
more swiftly away than it would have done otherwise.

I have often heard my grandmother tell with great interest the proceedings of former years. One instance, I

recollect, was this : that at one time when the state legislature met, a man of rather ordinary appearance
presented himself. The members viewed him and then
asked him if he was the choice of the people ? His answer was this : Sirs, I am the only man in my town ; of
course there was no one to set up against me ; therefore
I considered it my privilege to come here, and I have
made my appearance. This caused some glee, but the
honest man was not refused a seat. At another time, as
the military laws were in those days similar to ours, a
neighboring town legally warned a meeting for the purpose of choosing military officers and to have a training.
After the officers were chosen there was but one remaining soldier; and he, looking wishfully upon his superiors,
said : Gentlemen, I have one request to make, that is, as
I am the only soldier, I hope your honors will not be too
severe in drilling me, but will spare me a little as I may
be needed another time. He could form a solid column,
he said, but it racked him shockingly to display. At another time, when they were to have a training, an officer
went fifty miles to Lower Coos, as it was then called, or
Haverhill now, for two quarts of spirit, to treat his company with. As they had no carriages in those days,
neither had they a road suitable for one, he took his
horse, put on the saddle and then a pair of large saddle-
bags, filled with provisions for the journey, and a jug for
the spirit, and provender for his horse; and as they
traveled at that time, it took him three or four days to
perform this journey. When on his way home, by some
unknown accident, the cork got loose and the bottle was
emptied of its contents into the saddle bags. The liquor

would have been saved had not the oats soaked up a part of it; he, however, saved enough to treat his company with. They did not require so much then as too many have required since that time.

It had been a matter of considerable inquiry, how they should get a passage through the White Mountains. Two men who went in search, by name Timothy Nash and Benjamin Sawyer, discovered an opening through the Notch. One of them climbed a tree to be sure of the fact. Here one of them lost a mitten, it being on a high hill, and from that circumstance they gave it the name of the Mitten Mountain. When satisfied there might be a way found here to get to the fertile country on the Connecticut river, without going so far round, they gave the information, and were rewarded by having the whole tract of level land given them above the Notch, and it was granted to them by Governor Wentworth in 1773, as Nash and Sawyer's Location, upon condition that they should cut and make a good road through this tract of land, and cause five families to settle on it in five years. This land was surveyed by General Buckman, a deputy surveyor of public lands, then belonging to the Province, now State of New Hampshire; and they had got some families settled here, and the people had begun to settle in Conway and Bartlett, and likewise in Jefferson, all of whom had an example set them by Colonel Whipple, from Portsmouth, who, for years was a real father to them. He placed them on his land, and all they could raise, more than they needed for their families, he bought; and paid them honestly to even half a cent. He used to bring from Portsmouth a bag of half cents to make

change, for the purpose of being honest himself and trying to make his tenants honest. This little surplus of
grain was carefully laid up for the inhabitants in case of
their own need, or that of other persons who should move
in.

At one time, provisions in Bartlett were scarce, and
some of the people took their sacks and money in their
hands and came through the woods, a distance of not
less than thirty miles, to buy bread. This was refused
by the Colonel, saying his own inhabitants wanted all he
had; and they were obliged to return empty. They,
however, had the precaution to examine and find where
the grain was, and shortly afterward returned, and with
an auger, bored a hole up through the floor under where
the grain was, secured by a lock, held their sacks under,
and filled them. When satisfied they stopped the hole
with a plug, and then carried the filled sacks on their
backs to the woods, where they had handsleighs prepared to draw the grain, and thus returned in safety. The
Colonel finding it out, and being sensible of his error,
made but little fuss about it, yet took care how he dealt
with them afterward.

The inhabitants now while clearing the timber off their
lands, made ashes, which was boiled into salts, and ex-
changed for goods. Everything was very dear. As the
distance was so great to go round to get to the sea-
board, they began to contrive means to go to Portland,
or, perhaps, Portsmouth was the first place where they
went to market. With one horse fixed to a car, they first
went through the woods. The form of the car was sim-
ply this: two poles cut ten or fifteen feet in length, the

smaller ends serving as thills for the horse to draw by and the larger ends dragging on the ground, and fastened nearly in the middle with some short poles, on which they would place a bag, or other articles of loading. In this way they got along quite well until they came to the Notch. This was a trying place to get through. To go where they now do, was then utterly impossible. They then turned out at the top of the Notch and went over the edge and so managed to get to the top, and by taking a zigzag course, as much as possible, got down; but in doing this there was danger of the horse tipping over, the hill was so steep. And when they returned, they would tie a rope around the horse's neck, to keep him from falling backwards. At one time, however, one horse did so fall; but he was helped up without receiving much injury. At length a committee was chosen to search and look out the best road. They agreed in all places until they came to the Notch. There they held a council. One-half was for making the road on one side of the stream, and the other half, on the other side; but after considerable consultation on the subject, one of them turned and voted to make the road on the side of the Saco, where it is now. Reader, when you pass this place, now spoken of, please to look and judge for yourself, if you would devise a way to make a road on the other side of the stream, and then imagine what courage and perseverance our forefathers possessed. They never seemed to take hold of the plow and look back, but drove on.

At this time, grandfather remained at Guildhall. He had settled on a beautiful piece of land, easy to cultivate, on the Connecticut river, and things began to look flourishing. He seemed to be in a way to live without much hard labor himself, as his two eldest daughters were married, and his four sons growing up to help him. But in this easy situation he could not long remain. Having an ambitious, enterprising, public spirited disposition, and after going to market in the manner spoken of, and knowing there must be more help and perseverance to make this way practicable, he left his situation and volunteered once more to serve the public. In January, 1792, he took his family and moved to Nash and Sawyer's Location, bought out my father, who had some time before bought out three or four settlers who had declined to remain, and had been living there alone, keeping bachelor's hall in one of the small huts they had built.

Soon after this, my father rather than to be crowded by neighbors, moved twelve miles down the Saco river, where he would have elbow room enough; and then he began in the woods, in what is called Hart's Location, and remains there until this day, making as much improvement as possible, and laboring for the public good; while grandfather was beginning again in the woods, yea, more than the woods, in the valley of the Amanoosuc, surrounded by mountains on all sides. He afterward sold his farm at Guildhall, and the effects or proceeds he laid out in this lonesome spot, far from any neighbors, twelve miles either way. In a little log cabin they lived many years, suffering all the hardships which might well be expected or borne in this lonely, uncultivated place; and as they were dependent on their neighbors for food, they were obliged to go, or send their children that distance to obtain it, always feeling anxious for their safety when they were gone, fearing some accident might befall them. The way was so rough they were fearful the horse would break his leg and injure the child. Many an hour, I have heard my grandmother say, she has spent in meditation of her absent children; and many times, at a late hour in the night, before they would return; and then she would pour out her love in prayer and thankfulness to her heavenly Father for preserving them, and that she was permitted to receive them again to her humble mansion.

Thus they lived several years, working on their farms and making roads; sometimes for pay and sometimes without pay, just as it happened, until the Legislature saw fit to grant them a turnpike in 1803. This was divided into shares to the number of five hundred, and let out to different men to make. After a while, as traveling and business increased, he built a large and convenient two-story dwelling, on an elevated spot, on the west end of what has since been called Giant's Grave, with two rooms under ground. From the chamber in the second story, was an outside door, which opened so that one could walk out on the hill, which was beautiful, and gave a view of all the flat country around it. He built a large barn, stable, sheds and other out buildings, a saw mill and grist mill, etc.; the latter was of but little use, being one and a half miles from where he lived. The mice injured the bolt so much it was difficult to keep it in repair; but the saw mill was of great service, both to him and to my father, when building. Thus he prospered and lived well; but his children were not satisfied with their situation; married, and left him, one after another. Their leaving him and setting them off, put him in rather low circumstances in his advanced age; still, he had sufficient, but was in want of some one to help him, as will be shown in the next chapter.

CHAPTER II.

THE CRAWFORDS.

Ethan Allen Crawford was born in Guildhall, Vermont, in 1792, and when quite young, his parents moved to Hart's Location, in New Hampshire, twelve miles from neighbors, one way, and six the other; in a log house, in a small opening among the trees.

Here our family lived alone, with the exception of a hired man. One Saturday, my parents went to spend the sabbath in Bartlett, among the christians; and they left me and a brother older than I was with this hired man, to take care of us, and with a plenty of provisions to last until their return. Soon after they were gone, this man picked up such things as he thought valuable, and what victuals were cooked for us during their absence, started for the woods, and left us, two little boys (to use the words of Ethan), with none to keep us company all night, and without food. We had a cow, but neither of us was large enough to milk her. We, however, got some potatoes, roasted them in the ashes, and ate them; then, being tired and lonesome, we hugged ourselves up together and went to sleep. On Monday, when they came and found us, and things as they were, my father was so incensed with the man for his ill treatment to his little helpless children, that he followed him to Franconia, where he came out of the woods. We recovered some of the stolen articles, and had the man punished for his perfidy.

While my father was clearing up his land, I and my brother helped him all we could. Many times I have chopped, and my hands would swell and pain me in the night so much, that my mother would get up and poultice them, to give me ease. I never had a hat, a mitten, or a pair of shoes, of my own, that were made for me, until I was nearly thirteen years old. I could harness and unharness horses in the cold winter weather, with my head, hands and feet nearly bare, and not mind or complain of the cold, as I was used to it; it made me tough and healthy.

After this I was sent to school in the winter, to some one of the neighboring towns, wherever I could work night and morning, and help pay my board, until I could read, write and cipher.

In 1811, I enlisted as a soldier, under the command of Capt. Stark, for eighteen months; with a promise, from another officer, that I should have a commission after we should get to Plattsburgh. Here I staid through the summer; and late in the fall the spotted fever raged in the company, and I was one of the subjects of this contagious disease. I was sick, and did not know but that it was even unto death, as numbers were dying daily around me. I was carried to the hospital; but as it was so filled with the sick, I thought I would fare better in my own bunk, and got back there some how or other. Here I made the best I could of it, and having a strong constitution, as soon as my fever turned, I crawled out and bought me a turkey and had a part of it made into

broth, of which I took a little at a time until it strength-
ened me, and I could get about.

Thinking that if I staid there I would not live long, I
made an application for a furlough to go home, which
was granted me. I started, but was so weak and emaciated, I could walk but a short distance in a day, and
when the wind blew I was obliged to stop and lay by, as
I could not stand against it. I, however, succeeded in
getting home to the White Hills in fourteen days, with
the assistance of some kind friends, who would occasionally give me a ride. Once on the way I was suspected
of having run away from the army and I was obliged to
show my furlough.

In the winter, after regaining my health, I returned to
my duty. I afterward had to take the place of a Lieu-
tenant, a Sergeant and a Corporal, and as I was called
upon oftener than many others on duty, one day when I
was gone they chose their officers, and I was left out.
This dissatisfied me so much I made my complaints to
the man that had promised to raise me above a common
soldier. He wrote to Washington, to headquarters, and
we soon had an answer saying I might be discharged.
This I showed to the officer that had the authority to
give the discharge. He was unwilling; but after he had
done it, he gave me a Corporal's commission, which I accepted, and I stayed for a while. The main army moved
off, and I was left with a company of invalids, and
not much to do; I thought best to go home, and so I
went home.

In 1814, I hired with two men who had engaged to
take out the trees by the roots, and prepare for a road

sixteen feet wide, leading from Russell, in the State of
New York to St. Johns, for fifty cents a rod. We made
a beginning soon after the frost was out of the ground ;
took our provisions and cooking utensils with us, and
there, in those woods, I staid seven months without
once coming out. Three men of us, in that time, with
one yoke of oxen, grubbed and made a road nearly eight
miles long, and then I went home.

In the spring of 1815, as my eldest brother was in Russell, in the State of New York, and I having been there,
and liking the place, I concluded to go again. I bought
a horse, and went. The eighth and ninth of June, the
ground froze and the snow fell a foot deep or more, and
lasted for me to draw logs to a saw mill, two days, with
four oxen.

Here the pigeons were so numerous in some places, that
the farmers were obliged to watch their fields to keep
the birds from picking up the sowed grain. At one time
I went with three other men into the woods, on to a
swell or small ridge of land, where the pigeons had made
their nests and hatched their young ones, and on half
an acre of land, in some beech trees, we found them in
great abundance. We would chop one tree and fall it
against another and that would cause the young ones to
drop from both trees. Some trees had forty nests in
each of them, with two young ones in each nest. These
were a clear squad of fat, and as they could only hop
along and could not get out of our way, we picked them
up and pulled off their heads and took out their crops to
keep them from spoiling. There we worked until each of
us had as many as we could carry home in a bag, on a
horse's back; and a greater sight than that I never saw.

Among the numerous branches of business which the man I hired with had for me to do, was working on a river of swift water, where we boated barrels of potash fifteen miles down the river. These barrels weighed five hundred apiece. I could take one of these at a time, of this average weight, and put it into the boat, hoisting it two feet. There was but one other man in the boat that could lift more than one end of a barrel. My strength was so great, and my health so good, I did not know but it would last, until I began to have the rheumatism, by being so often and so much exposed, and in the heat of the day and when in a state of perspiration, obliged to go into the water, and remain there as we oftentimes had to do.

Here I lived, and had bought me a piece of land in the town of Louisville, in the State of New York, and I had made a handsome beginning, intending to settle there, near this brother of mine; when, in 1816, we received a letter from our aged grandfather, desiring one of us to come and live with him. He said he would not live long, being troubled with a cancer on his under lip; that his children were all married and settled away from him, such as were capable of taking care of the harvests; and that one of us should have a deed of all his property, if he would come and see him, grandmother and Uncle William, their eldest son (who was not capable of managing his business through life), and pay his grandfather's honest debts.

My brother, who was always considered the wiser of us two, said he would not do this, and advised me not to; setting forth the many difficulties that would arise on the part of near relatives, who, though not willing to go there themselves, yet might find fault with another's going; and the great responsibility resting upon the one who should undertake the care of old people. Although he honored and respected them, yet he felt inadequate to the task, and thought it devolved upon some one better qualified for it. This counsel I heard and concluded to abide by.

Unfortunately, I got lame and could not work; I therefore thought I would go home and visit them and my parents who lived twelve miles distant from them; and, in December, I started. On my arriving there, the old gentleman expressed marks of gratitude for my obedience to his summons but as I had made up my mind according to my brother's advice, I told him I had not come to stay, only to see him. On hearing this he put his hand upon my shoulder and entreated me in such a manner, with tears trickling down his furrowed cheeks, that my former resolution was shaken; for he had ever been a kind grandparent to me, and how could I deny him my services now when he so much needed them?

I then concluded to go back to Louisville and sell my possessions there, and return to their assistance, and do the best I could for them. Accordingly, I went back and sold, and in March, 1817, returned to them again. I brought with me two hundred and eighty dollars which I had earned. This I contributed to the benefit of the farm. Then I gave my notes for a sum of from two to three thousand dollars, and took up his. Afterward he gave me a deed of his farm, by me giving them a mortgage back, for their maintenance through life. I provided every means which he and his friends thought proper, to remove the disease, but to no purpose, it was so far advanced it was incurable.

* It was now necessary to have a nurse, one who would feel an interest in his being made comfortable, as the disorder so much affected grandmother she could not dress it, neither could she bear to stay in the room when it was being dressed. And they desired me to go for a cousin of mine, by the name of Lucy, who was a particular favorite of theirs, and get her to come and take care of him. I went and obtained her consent, with that of her parents, who well knew his situation, and felt anxious that his last days might be made as comfortable and easy as possible.

The 5th of May, Lucy came home with me and took the whole care of grandfather; and he was so well pleased with what she did for him, that he thought no one else could do for him as well; and would never let his own children dress his lip when she was there. His pains, which were severe, he bore like a christian, without a murmur or a groan, when awake, and he would frequently say he had no more laid upon him than he was able to bear. He would converse upon death with as much freedom as though he was going to take a long journey into a far country, and never expected to return.

He gave Lucy and myself a great many counsels, and expressed a desire, in the course of the summer, that as Lucy took such good care of him, he hoped she would unite with me, and continue there to stay; and, in the like manner, rock the cradle for the declining years of grandmother, as she did for him; and likewise for Uncle

William, who, he said, might cause some trouble, as most people in his situation possess a quick disposition, and would sometimes be irritable. He told us not to mind such things but to discharge a clear conscience toward him, and we should have a reward for it, and if no other, we should have a peace of mind, which would surpass everything in this world. He would often say to Lucy when his cancer increased so much as to become an inhabited corruption, that he was only a glass for others to look into and see their own final corruption at death. He would never suffer any one to sit up with him, or even go into his room in the night to ask if he wanted anything; always seeming to be afraid we should do so much for him that we should get sick. In this way he lived from May until September upon nothing but sweetened milk and water, with sometimes a little spirit in it, which he said he could not well do without, as the cancer in his mouth and throat was so offensive to him. When his flesh was all gone, and his teeth fell into his mouth, his spirit left his body, without a struggle or a groan, with his hands and eyes uplifted toward heaven ; he, by signs, commended Uncle William and grandmother to my care. Our good neighbors, who lived at a distance of twelve and twenty miles, assembled and paid their respects to his remains, on the 27th.

As Lucy had with so much judgment, alacrity and perseverance discharged her duty toward grandfather, and knowing no other that would fill her place, I solicited her to engage with me in the performance of the remaining obligations I was then under. She accordingly agreed to, after I should have obtained the consent of her parents, and on the first of November, we were married. She now became a partaker of all my joys and sorrows.

In the winter of 1818, being in good health, and possessing a goodly share of strength, I, with the help of Uncle William, managed to do all our own work, without having any other help, as we wished to economize all we could to meet my notes and take them up when they should become due. In this way our honest endeavors were prospered; and I was able to make my first payment without trouble, and after getting through with my spring work, in the summer I hired men and went to labor on the turnpike, for pay, laying up everything we could earn and save from our common, necessary living, for that purpose, as I was determined to pay every demand as soon as it should be called for.

CHAPTER III.

EARLY on the morning of the 18th of July, my family not being well, I went to our nearest neighbors for some assistance. It was nearly eight o'clock when I returned with Mrs. Rosebrook, and not long after we had a son born, which weighed nearly five pounds. After doing what was necessary to be done at the house, at eleven o'clock I went to carry some dinner to our men who were at work on the Cherry Mountain road, one and a half miles from home. Grandmother desired me, on my return, to bring her some trout, as she said I must give them a good treat and do something extra for their services and my good fortune that morning. I accordingly, though reluctantly, obeyed her commands. The trout were in as great haste for the hook as I was for them. I caught in a few minutes, a fine string of good large sized ones. I was gone about one hour from home, and when on my return, the first sight which caught my eyes as I came out of the woods, was flames of fire ascending the tops of the chimneys, ten or fifteen feet in the air! I added a new speed to my horse, who was then under a good headway, and I was soon there. Here I found Lucy and her infant placed on some feather beds behind an old blacksmith's shop, where she could not see the flames of fire in the open air. I passed her immediately by and flew to the house, and tried to save something from it, but all in vain, the fire was raging, and to that height I

34

could not save a hive of bees, which stood a few rods
from it. These were suffered to perish. There were no
men there excepting a Mr. Boardman, from Lancaster,
who, with his wife, on their return home from Saco,
called for some refreshments, and while this was preparing, Mrs. Boardman came into the room and inquired of
Lucy how she did, and what she should say to her mother
who lived three miles from them, when she should get
home. After a little conversation and receiving thanks
from Lucy for her kindness, she took her leave and went
out. The room where Lucy lay was about ten feet wider
than the other part of the house, which was built with
these two rooms under ground. And there was a large
poplar whose boughs and leaves touched the chamber
window where grandmother slept. While in conversation with Mrs. Boardman Lucy saw smoke and leaves
pass her window; but as she was much engaged and the
wind shifted, she forgot to mention it. The girl, going
into one of the rooms, heard the crackling of fire over-
head, and when she opened the chamber door, the flames
met her. She immediately closed the door and gave information. In a few minutes Mrs. Boardman returned
and said, Mrs. Crawford, do not be frightened, the house
is on fire and cannot be saved; be quiet and keep still,
you shall be taken care of; remember your life is of more
value than all the property which is to be consumed.
These words, coming in so friendly a manner, and from
so good a woman, calmed all her fears, and, when left
alone, she had the presence of mind to command herself
without trembling. She arose and dressed herself, then
went to the desk, which stood in the room, unlocked it,

took out all the papers and other things of consequence
from the drawers, and put them in a pine chest, which
stood near by, then asked Mr. Boardman to save it, which
he did. She then went into another room and took out
some drawers, and they were carried out and saved.
She would have taken down the top of a brass clock, had
it not been for Mrs. Boardman, who would, every time
she saw her making exertions, admonish her by saying
she was not aware of her critical situation, and as it
hindered her by these arguments from doing much herself, Lucy gave up and was placed in an arm chair, and
carried to the place where I found her. The infant was
the last thing taken from the burning ruins, as Mrs. Rosebrook had taken it and laid it upon a bench in the bar-
room, for the house was built for a tavern. Mr. B. asked where it was? She said she knew, and ran in and
brought it out. We had a pig shut up in a pen so near
the building, that before he could make his escape, was
burned. The noise of this pig attracted the attention of
the other hogs and brought them to the place, and it was
with difficulty that Lucy and one little brother of hers,
four years old, who lived with us, could keep them from
tearing everything to pieces. Beds all on fire—cheeses
all around—hogs in the midst of them—all hurly burly ;
while the female party had much to do to keep safe
what they had taken from the house, and Mr. Boardman had his horse and chaise to look after. As there
was but little help, there could not be much saved. The
day was fair, and the wind strong, and it blew in different directions, so that the bed on which Lucy lay caught
fire three times, which she extinguished by smothering it
with her hands.

The fire is supposed to have communicated from a candle, accidentally left burning in a kitchen chair, in the morning, in a tightly ceiled room, by our grandmother; and it was some time making its appearance, owing to the stillness of the air, as that was the place where it was discovered. Lucy having been unwell in the night, the old lady was called upon to come and see her, and after rendering her services, Lucy was better and desired her to go to bed again. This, she was at first unwilling to do; but after a little persuading, she went. I gave her a new long candle, which she took and set in the chair, and then she lay down on the bed, not thinking to sleep, as she said; but she did fall asleep, and when she awoke, the sun shone brightly in her face, and thinking she had neglected Lucy, and unmindful of the candle, left it burning; coming out of the room, she shut the door after her and came down stairs.

Dear reader, my feelings at this time, may better be imagined than described; no inhabited house within six miles, on one side, and twelve the other, my family in this destitute situation, all my carriages sharing the same fate with the buildings, and no means to convey them hence. As Mrs. Boardman was a feeble woman, and out of health, she could not think of giving up her chaise to carry away my family with; neither was it a desirable carriage for them. And while we were contriving some means to get them away, it seemed as though directed by the hand of Providence, a tin peddler happened along, and after we had put what things we saved into an old barn which stood at such a distance from the other buildings that it escaped the fire, he kindly emptied

his cart of its contents in the field, and we placed some
feather beds in his cart and put Lucy and her brother and
the babe in it. I then gave the before mentioned trout
to Mr. Boardman, helped them to their carriage, and they
went their way, and we went ours. While on the way,
the baby was uneasy, and Mrs. Rosebrook picked rasp-
berries and gave them to the child, and to its mother.
Grandmother and Mrs. Rosebrook on horseback, myself
and the peddler on foot, made up our traveling party,
and about the setting of the sun, and over a very rough
road, we all arrived in safety at Mrs. Rosebrook's. The
two girls we had living with us, staid and slept in the
barn, and likewise the men, when they returned from
work. I had laid in a good store of provisions for my
family's use, as we were not always sure of a crop, and
depended on buying. We had a small store pretty well
filled with salt and salt fish. I had bought forty dollars
worth of wheat and forty of pork. I had made two-
thirds of a barrel of maple sugar, and when done sugar-
ing, had taken the large potash kettle which I had used
and brought across the Amanoosuc river, I walking over
on a log, the kettle on my head, Uncle William helping
me to put the kettle on my head; after putting it in a cart
I brought it home. These and all other kinds of provisions were destroyed. Some new cheese, however, was
saved; this was in the furthermost part of the house,
where the fire came last. All my farming tools were destroyed, excepting those that the men had working with,
such as plows, harrows, hoes, shovels, rakes, pitchforks,
scythes, etc. In the morning we had enough and to
spare; in the evening, nothing left but this new cheese,
and the milk of the cows.

CHAPTER IV.

THE next day was the Sabbath; the horses were sent for, and the girls came down and joined us. One incident, by the way, I would just relate. The swallows, after losing their nests, followed the family, and the barns of Mr. Rosebrook seemed to be alive with them; they were actually partakers of our trouble.

Monday, my parents and Lucy's came to see what was to be done; and they agreed to move a small house, twenty-four feet square, which belonged to me, one and a half miles from where ours stood before it was burned; and sent an invitation to our neighbors, who immediately collected, with provisions for themselves and oxen, to draw the building.

My loss by the fire was estimated at $3,000, and there was no insurance. I was young and ambitious, but this shock of misfortune almost overcame me; and I was for some days quite indifferent which way the world went. I at length was constrained to arouse my feelings, and once more put my shoulder to the wheel.

My house was placed upon the spot, and left, with one outside door, and chimney up as high as the chamber floor; there were no windows and there was nothing but a rough, loose floor to walk upon. Yet we could not prevail upon Lucy to stay any longer than two weeks where she was. We therefore spread bedclothes for a carpet, and hung some up for a partition, to keep her from taking cold; and, thus situated, she was accidentally visited by several gentlemen and ladies from Portland. They seemed to sympathize with her, and afterward sent her several articles of furniture for the table. Lucy, however, took cold, which caused her some pain and trouble; and she was obliged to go back to Mr. Rosebrook's and remain there three weeks longer.

I hired two joiners, and went twelve miles for lumber, to work with, and while we were thus engaged, Colonel Binney, from Boston, with two young men, came along, by the way of Littleton, to my place. Finding us so destitute of everything, they staid but a short time, and then went down to father's. The young men wanted to go on the mountain; they consulted him, and agreed to take him for a guide, with a man to carry provisions and other necessary things. They rode to the top of the Notch, then sent back their carriage, and proceeded to the woods. They had much difficulty in managing to get through; they, however, proceeded slowly; sometimes crawling under a thicket of trees, sometimes over logs and windfalls, until they arrived where they could walk on the top of trees. This may seem to some strange, but it is nevertheless true. They never reached the summit but managed to get along on some of the hills.

As the day was growing to a close, they returned to the woods, in order to pass the night, and erected a shelter for their protection. A dense fog arose and during the night it rained. In the morning, owing to the darkness, they could not tell the best way to proceed, but took the surest way, by following the Amanoosuc river, and came to my house. These men wore fine and costly garments into the woods, but when they returned, their clothes were torn and much injured by the brush, and their hats looked as if they had been through a beggar's press. They were much exposed all night, without fire or food.

In September, there came two gentlemen to my father's, and engaged him to go with them to the top of Mount Washington, where they placed an inscription in Latin, which was engraved on a brass plate, and nailed it on a rock; they likewise filled a bottle and put it in a rock. The inscription was as follows, as I had it copied and kept carefully at home. (I vouch not for the Latin or translation being correct; it is at all events, a true copy, as found on the plate; and was translated, with the exception of the word "*perspire*," by a friend, who was afterward in the vicinity.)

"*Altius ibunt, qui ad summa nitunteer*"—They will go higher who strive to enter heaven. "*Nil reputans, si quid superesset agendum*"—Think nothing done while anything remains to be done. "*Sic itur ad astra.*"—We go thus to the stars. "*Stinere facto per inhostales sylvas Rustribus pramptis feliciter superrtes. (Eheu quantus adest vius sudor!) Johannes Brazer, Cantabrigsensis, Georgius Dawson, Philadelphiensis, hic posuerant ivid Septembris MDCCCXVIII.*" After passing inhospitable woods, and surmounting abrupt ledges (how it made us perspire), John Brazer, of Cambridge, and George Dawson, of Philadelphia, placed this inscription here on the fourth day of the Ides of September, 1818.

We succeeded in having a comfortable, small house, for the winter 1819. We had now many difficulties to encounter, owing to the limited size of our small house; it being at that time the principal, if not the only market road then traveled by the people, who depended upon going to market in the winter with their produce, from the upper part of New Hampshire, and even west of Vermont; and the snow did not fall early to make a good sleigh path. When it did, our house was filled, and Lucy would many times have to make a large bed on the floor for them to lie down upon, with their clothes on, and I would build a large fire in a large rock or stone chimney, that would keep them warm through the night. It was no uncommon thing to burn in that fire-place a cord of wood in twenty-four hours, and sometimes more.

At this time my father thought it best to sell, as there was a chance, he thought; he being holden with me on the notes, I suppose, would like to have been liberated from them. He consulted with grandmother, and gave her and William a mortgage of his farm, at that time worth two of mine, so that there should be no incumbrance on my barn. But the man to whom we expected to sell, drew back, and we still remained, and struggled along as well as we could, through the winter.

In the month of May four gentlemen came on horseback to visit the mountains. I gave them the best information I could. They set off together, and made the best they could of their excursion through the forests, but suffered considerable inconvenience by the thickness of the trees and brush, which would every now and then take hold of their clothes, and stop them; they returned well satisfied, notwithstanding the unfriendly brush.

As this was the third party which had visited the

mountains since I came here to live, we thought it best to cut a path through the woods; accordingly my father and I made a foot path from the Notch out through the woods, and it was advertised in the newspapers, and we soon began to have a few visitors. As my accommodations were limited, small parties were under the necessity of stopping at my father's, eight miles from the Notch.

This summer I succeeded in removing a barn from the place where our house had been brought by our neighbors, after the fire, and I converted the barn into a stable for horses. We considered it quite comfortable for the winter, and as I had payments to make, I had to work economically to be able.

I spent the winter of 1820 in doing my own work and assisting the traveler up and down the Notch, and over the mountains toward Lancaster. As it is a common thing for the wind to sweep away the snow through the Notch, opening and leaving it bare, so the teamsters required help to get along, and sometimes they have been obliged to leave a part of their loads at the Notch House, and I have gone down there and taken it and conveyed it to the owners, and on my return would bring home grain and other necessary things for our use, as I ever calculated to manage so as to load both ways, and not lose my time or the wear of my horses for nothing.

In March, as I had a famous dog for catching deer, I told Lucy one pleasant morning, I was going out to the Notch with my dog, and I hoped to bring a deer home, alive, and we would tame him. She smiled and said to me, she thought I had better give up such an idea as that, for who could catch and halter-break a wild animal like a deer. Never mind, said I, there is nothing like trying. So I took my rope, dog and snow-shoes, and commenced my journey. After traveling about four miles in the roads, I turned out and went into the woods, say half a mile, when Watch, my dog, gave an alarm, which told me he had found a deer. I went as fast as I could and told Watch to be careful and not hurt the deer. He had found a young buck and stopped him; I went up and Watch took him by the ear, and held him, while I tied on my rope in form of a halter, and then began to descend the hill, and come into the road. He was rather turbulent at first, but soon became quite tame and peaceable, and would smell of my hands, as I perspired some, as if for salt. I brought him home, and made a place in the stable and put him in, and Lucy's little brother fed him with cabbage and small pieces of cut potatoes. We kept him until June, when by accident, the little boy happened to leave one whole potato, which got so far into his throat, that I could not remove it, and consequently the poor thing died.

In May, there came a gentleman and lady, and put up with us, for the night; it began to snow, and in the morning the snow was good twelve inches deep; and they being in a hurry, were desirous to proceed on their journey, but did not know how they could get through the snow with their wagon. I then brought up my horse sled, took off the wheels from their wagon, and placed them and the wagon on the sled, and prepared a seat for each of us to ride comfortably, attached my horse to the sled, and carried them to Bethlehem, twelve miles. As we had now got out of the snowy region, and they could travel by themselves, I assisted in putting their carriage together again, for which he gave me a dollar, and we took our leave of each other, and they pursued their way and I returned home. I went one and a half miles down the Amanoosuc river, or Ompompanusuck, according to the ancient Indian name, and took the frame of an old grist mill, which stood there useless, and which belonged to me, and brought it home, having taken it apart, and made a temporary cheese house, and had a dairy, and made twelve hundred weight of cheese, which I carried to market in the fall, and sold for a good price. This enabled me to make another payment of $200.

This summer there came a considerable large party of distinguished characters, such as the author of the New Hampshire map, etc., to my house, about noon, to ascend the mountains and give names to such hills as were un-named, and after a dinner of trout, they set out, taking me for a guide and baggage-carrier. We rode to the Notch, and there I was loaded equal to a pack-horse, with cloaks and necessary articles for two nights, with a plenty of what some call " Black Betts," or " O-be-joy-ful," as it was the fashion in those days, to make use of this kind of stuff, and especially upon such occasions. We traveled on until we reached the camp, about three miles from the road, then I struck up a fire, cut wood, and prepared our usual supper, spread our blankets, brought for that purpose, and after some interesting sto-ries told by the party, I believe we all fell asleep. In the morning, after breakfast, we started on our intended ex-pedition, taking only provisions enough for the day, and a sufficient quantity of " O-be-joyful," and set forward and went over several hills, and came to a beautiful pond of clear water, distant one mile from the apex of the hill. Here we made a stop for some time, enjoying the water, which was delicious, and then went to the summit of Mount Washington. There they gave names to several peaks, and then drank healths to them in honor to the great men whose names they bore, and gave toasts to them; and after they had all got through, they put it upon me to do the same; but as this was a new thing to me, and not being prepared, I could only express my feelings by saying I hoped all of us might have good success and return to our respective families in safety, and find them in health; which was answered by a cheer from all, as they had cheered at other times before, when any one had drank a toast. The day was fine, and our feelings seemed to correspond with the beauties of the day, and after some hours had swiftly passed away in this manner, we concluded to leave this grand and magnificent place and return to a lower situation on earth. We then left the hill, and came down to the before mentioned pond. Here we staid a long time partaking of its waters, until some of us became quite blue, and from this circumstance we agreed to give it the name of Blue Pond, and at rather a late hour we left it and proceeded toward the camp, but did not all arrive there until nine o'clock in the evening. This water so much troubled one of our party, or the elevated situation on which we traveled, fatigue, or some other cause, had such an effect upon him that he could not get along without my assistance; and he being a man of two hundred weight, caused me to make use of all my strength, at times. I, however, managed to get down at last, and when I did, I was so tired, I prostrated myself upon the ground and told them I could do no more that night, they must look out for themselves, for I was tired to the very bone. They cut some wood and did the best they could that night, and in the morning, sleep had again restored us, so that after taking some refreshment, we started for home, where we all arrived in safety, and in good spirits. Here we with pleasure recalled the proceedings of the previous day, and partaking of another dinner, most of them returned to their places of residence the same day.

In September, at one time, there came a number of gentlemen up through the Notch, and sent to me to prepare and furnish them with provisions and other necessaries for the expedition. I was accordingly fitted out, and when ready, my pack weighed eighty pounds. I carried it to the Notch on horseback, and when I arrived there the sun was setting, and the party had taken the path and gone along and left their cloaks by the way for me. I piled them on top of my load and budged on as fast as possible, and when I arrived at the camp it was dusk; there was no fire; wood was to be chopped, and supper to prepare, and when all this was done, I was tired enough to sleep without being rocked in a cradle.

In November I went on the hill in front of my house, south, and there set up a short line of sable traps, twenty-three in number, and caught twenty-five sables of fine quality, and one black cat, or fisher.

The winter of 1821 I spent doing my own work and buying salt, and transporting it from Portland to Lancaster, and exchanging it with the merchants for grain and other things for my family's use. And as I had been somewhat unlucky with my pet deer last summer, I thought to try again for another, and in a manner like the former one, I prepared and went near the same place. I found several, one of which I took alive. This was a beautiful young doe and she was with young. I now felt quite rich in taking this prize. I suppose my feelings were similar to those spoken of by Robinson Crusoe, when he succeeded in taking the llamas on the island. I did not know but that they might increase; we could build a park and keep them, as these animals are easily tamed, and then I should have them to show our visitors in the summer when they came. Perhaps I could now and then spare one for the table, if requested by them; but alas! this was only imaginary, like the fable of the maid and her milk pail. I put on my rope in the same manner as I did the former one, and began to try to lead her, but I could do nothing with her; she would not walk with me, so I shouldered her and brought her into the road; this made quite a load for me to travel with, as I was then four miles from home; but said I to myself, without some pain there will be no gain; so I made the best I could of it, and when in the road would often set her down and try to lead her, but I could not. This was not exactly like the one I had taken the preceding year, it was of a dark brown color. After I got her home, I had either hurt her in bringing her home, or she was so delicate she would not partake of food, and to put her out of misery, I concluded we had better dress her. This was as fine a piece of venison as I had ever seen. Now as I had not saved this one's life, I said I would go again ; so I went and my dog started a good sized buck, and followed him toward home, and near the road he had stopped him, and then waited for me to come up and take him, and while there they were observed by some travelers passing along at this time, before I had time to come up with him, although I made long strides on my snow-shoes, as I feared something would happen to him. When I came up, I found the traveler had been to the house and obtained a gun and shot him, and to my great mortification I found him dead, with the man exulting in triumph over this great feat which he had performed. I then told him the great disappointment which he had unconsciously given me ; but as he was dead, it was of no use to make many words about it, so he helped me to bring him home, and here he was served like the former one, and sent to Portland.

In March, I hired Esquire Stuart to come with his compass and go into the woods, and see if there could not be a better and more practicable way found to ascend the mountains. We set out with provisions, blankets, fire-works, and snow-shoes for the woods. We set our compass, and spotted trees, which made a line to be followed at another time. When night came on, I built a camp and struck up a fire. We ate our supper and retired with our dog quietly to rest. We spent three days in making this search, and returned well satisfied we had found the best way ; for the road which we had heretofore traveled was an uneven one, going up a hill and then down again, and this in so many successions, that it made it tiresome to those who were not accustomed to this kind of jour-

3

neying. The way which we had now found was over a comparatively level surface for nearly seven miles, following the source of the Amanoosuc, or Ompompanusuck, until we arrived at the foot of Mount Washington, and then taking a ridge or spur of the hill. We could now ascend without much difficulty, and found there might be a road made, with some expense, sufficiently good, so that we might ride this seven miles, which we thought would facilitate the visitor very much in his progress; and, to add to my encouragement, some gentlemen from Boston made a subscription in 1823 to this purport : that, providing I should make a good carriage road, and have it passable in three years, they would be holden to pay the sums which were set against their respective names; and we had nearly $200 subscribed for this purpose ; but as I was already under so much embarrassment I did not feel able to build an addition to my house, and I well knew that if I made this road, and did not have suitable accommodations for those who would be likely to come, it would only be imposing upon the public to have a road to the mountain and not have house room enough to make those comfortable who came to stay with us. I, therefore, was obliged to give up this generous offer of theirs, and at my own expense do what I could from one year to another; but still intending to do everything in my power to make all happy as possible in my humble situation.

In the summer, just before haying, I hired men and went with them to cut this path, and while in the woods, at the distance of three miles from home, as I was standing on an old log chopping, with my axe raised, the log

broke, and I came down with such force that the axe
struck my right ankle and glanced, nearly cutting my heel
cord off; I.bled freely, and so much so that I was unable to stand or go. The men that were with me, one a
brother of mine, and another stout man, took the cloths
we had our dinner wrapped in, and tied up my wound as
well as they could, and then began to contrive means to
get me out of the woods. They cut a round pole, and
with their frocks which they wore tied me in underneath
it, and thought they could carry me in like manner as we
bring dead bears through the woods; but in this way I
could not ride. They then let me down, and took turns
in carrying me on their backs, until we got out of the
woods; and then one of them came home and got a
horse, upon whose back I was helped; and I thus rode
home with both feet on one side in ladies' fashion,
and when I arrived there I was assisted in alighting.
There happened to be at my house then, a Mrs. Stalbard,
who is known in our country and bore the name of
Granny Stalbard, whose head was whitened with more
than eighty years; who ought to be remembered for the
good she had done, and many sufferings and hardships
she endured to assist others in distress, and who seemed
to be raised for the same end for which she lived in those
days. She was an old Doctress woman; one of the first
female settlers in Jefferson, and she had learned from the
Indians the virtues of roots and herbs, and the various
ways in which they could be made useful. Now the old
lady said it was best to examine this wound and have it
properly dressed; but as it had stopped bleeding I
told her I thought it better to let it remain as it then

was; but she thinking she was the elder, and knew better, unwrapped it, and it soon set bleeding afresh, and it was with difficulty she now stopped it. She, however, went into the field, plucked some young clover leaves, pounded them in a mortar, and placed them on my wound; this stopped the blood so suddenly that it caused me to faint; this was a new thing to me—a large stout man to faint!—which made me feel rather queerly, but there was no help for it. This wound laid me up pretty much the rest of the summer, but still we persevered, and these men, with some others, finished cutting the path through the woods. So it is that men suffer various ways in advancing civilization, and through God, mankind are indebted to the labors of men in many different spheres of life.

CHAPTER V.

This fall Captain Partridge came with a number of Cadets to ascend the mountain, and as I was not able to walk, we were under the necessity of sending for our nearest neighbor, Mr. Rosebrook, to guide them; and likewise at other times, we were obliged to send for him to guide gentlemen up the hills.

At this time, there was to be a general muster at Lancaster, and as I was lame, and not able to walk, Lucy was anxious to visit her parents in Guildhall, just opposite that place, and we concluded to go and see them; and on the day appointed, I, with others, went to see the soldiers perform; and while I was sitting down on the ground, there came a man who was celebrated for wrestling, and laid hold of me, and stumped me to throw him. I eased him off, and then he went to others in the same way, and received similar treatment, until he upset a whole row of old men sitting on a rail fence or board. He came again, and insisted upon my taking hold with him. I told him I was not in the habit of that kind of sport, and also, I was lame, and could not, if I had a disposition to; and he came the third time and caught hold of my vest and rent it several inches in length, and at the same time with his foot gave me such a blow on my lame ankle, that the hurt raised my temper to such a degree, that, unconscious of what I did, I put my fist in such an attitude that it laid him prostrate on the ground. He was taken up with rather a disfigured face; for which I was immediately sorry, for I knew he was influenced by liquor; but it was done, and many were glad of it, while I was ashamed to think I had given way to passion, and when I came to where Lucy was, I asked her to forgive my imprudence by mending my vest. I told her it should be the last time I would give way to an angry passion, and I have thus far kept my word.

In August 31, 1821, there came three young ladies, the Misses Austin, who were formerly from Portsmouth, to ascend the hills, as they were ambitious and wanted to have the honor of being the first females who placed their feet on this high, and now celebrated, place, Mount Washington. They were accompanied by their brother and Charles J. Stewart, Esq., who was then engaged to one of them, and married her, July 4, 1822, and Mr. Faulkner, who was then a tenant on their farm in Jefferson, attending with their baggage. They were provided with everything necessary for the expedition, and set forward. They went as far as the first camp that night, dividing it into two apartments, and then put up. The next morning they pursued their way until they reached the next camp, which they in like manner divided. It came on unfavorable weather, and now being in pretty good quarters, they staid and waited for a better prospect. And as their store of provisions began to fall short, Mr. Faulkner came in and said that I must, if I possibly could, go and relieve him, as he had grain out in the field, then suffering, and they wished to have me accompany them.

I now mustered all my courage, as I was then lame,

took a load on my back and a cane in my hand to help my lame foot, which was now healed over, and went and overtook them. The weather also looking favorable, we ascended at six o'clock in the morning, and reached the summit just as the sun had got to the meridian. What a beautiful sight! We could look over the whole creation with wonder and surprise, as far as the eye could extend, in every direction, and view the wonderful works of God! Every large pond and sheet of water was plain to be seen, within the circuit of one hundred miles, for some time, until the sun had got up so high as to cause a vapor to rise from the waters; this, also, was grand to see; the commencement of the little vapor, which would grow larger and larger, until it made a cloud and entrenched the view. Houses and farms were to be seen at a dis_tance, so far off that they appeared nothing more than small specks. At one time, previous, when here with some gentlemen, we counted forty-two different ponds in different directions. The Sebago Pond is distinctly to be seen, and some have thought they could see the ocean from this place; but as there is no object beyond, it appears to look like a cloud, differing only a trifle in color from the sky. The ladies returned, richly paid for their trouble, after being out five days and three nights. I think this act of heroism ought to confer an honor on them, as everything was done with so much prudence and modesty by them; there was not left a trace or even a chance for a reproach or slander excepting by those who thought themselves outdone by these young ladies.

The winter of 1822, as my ankle was weak, and the rheumatism now found its way to it, I staid at home as

much as possible, doing only what necessity really compelled me to, and in the spring I made a considerable
improvement on my mountain road. That summer I
went on the mountain with one gentleman, and as he was
a good traveler, we reached the top of the mountain
and returned to the camp before sunset. He proposed
coming home that night, so we took some refreshments
and started, and came along until it grew quite dark, and
I proposed to take a little nap and wait for the moon to
rise and give us some light. He hesitated a little in consequence of the wild beasts, which he said might happen
along, and take us while sleeping. I advised him to calm
his fears for my faithful dog would keep watch. We
took our blankets and lay down and soon fell asleep.
Presently there came a large bear spattering along in full
speed, and as the air came along with him he did not perceive us until within a few feet of us, and then the dog
sprang up and went after him; this awakened us, and as
the moon had now got up so high as to shine among the
trees, we could pursue our path quite well, and arrived
home about twelve o'clock.

We set traps, and caught two at one time, and some
more at other times this season, from which we obtained
considerable oil.

In August we had some young gentlemen from a Uni-
versity. They were preparing for the ministry, and as
they needed exercise, and a respite from their studies,
they chose this place to spend their leisure hours, and
regain their strength, and view and contemplate upon
the works of God, and climb the mountain. I went
with them as guide, and on the way I tried to shorten
the distance, and make their toil less tiresome by some

anecdotes, and telling some little stories; but as this did not coincide with their feelings, I gave up these trifles, and remained silent most of the way ; and when arriving at the summit, they on this high and elevated spot offered prayers to Almighty God for his goodness. This was, I think, the first prayer I ever heard on this mountain. This appeared solemn—now so high in the air, where we could look down upon inferior objects—what could be more interesting?

The same month others came, and among them was a sea-captain, a man of good stature and heavy ; he, while coming down from the hill, and in the act of jumping from one stone to another, lying there promiscuously, slipped, and unfortunately sprained his ankle. This was some trouble to him the rest of the way; however, he managed to get home. This was the greatest injury happening to any person while going up or coming down the hills, to my knowledge, during our stay at the White Mountains.

This summer we had some trouble with Uncle William, as brother had predicted, when he told me if I should go up there I must expect trouble from near relatives. As our situation was so uncomfortable, grandmother was under the necessity of making my father's house her home, and she was desirous of having William live with her ; yet she did not complain of his being ill treated, but wanted him, and coaxed him to go there and live with her. But he did not stay long, as they could do without him. They advised him to come home again, but this was contrary to the old lady's feelings, and she then advised him to go and live with his broth-

3*

er, and as he had ever been at her command, he obeyed her, and went. But this was not home to him; and after a while he returned, and said he would not be controlled any more, but would remain on his farm; he therefore came back, and received from us as good treatment as he ever had done.

In September, as I was ascending the mountain with two young gentlemen, we saw in the path, at some distance from the camp, a large bear's track, but saw nothing of the bear. On our descent, near this place, the dog left us, and in a few minutes went to barking in great earnest. I said, he has something. I went a few steps, and saw a cub, the bigness of a good-sized cur dog, climbing a tree. How we could get him was the next thing. We talked it over, and agreed that one should stand in the road and keep watch for the old one, whom we expected, should she hear the cries of her cub, and the other should climb the tree, and get him off, while I and the dog should remain at the foot of the tree and take him. The cub was followed up the tree in good style. He then walked out on a limb, and from that into a small tree, which I took hold of, and shook so hard that he fell off, and the dog caught him. I then took hold of him, and tying his mouth with my handkerchief, brought him safely home, and kept him some time. At length a hired man set up a pole, and tied a leather strap around his neck, and gave him a trough of water to bathe in. This he enjoyed remarkably well for a while, but when the strap stretched he slipped out his head, and said, I suppose, good day.

This winter, 1822, I spent in buying salt, and transporting it from Portland to Colebrook, and exchanging it

for grain; I likewise bóught a nice mare, for which I paid
in salt. I transported the salt with this mare by sleigh
loads. This winter my dog caught a great many deer,
and would go with any one who desired him; but an
enemy wanted him, and as he could not have him, because he was engaged, he gave him poison; and I lost my
famous dog. But shortly after, I bought another equally
as good.

In June, when returning from the camp, in company
with two young gentlemen, as we were traveling along,
we saw a bunch of mountain ash; they stopped, and each
cut for himself a beautiful, nice and straight cane, which
they intended to carry home with them; and after this
was done, we again pursued our path, I forward, and
they after me, in Indian file, as this was the manner in
which we used to travel. The one behind saw another
bunch, from which he thought he could select a better
cane. He stopped to cut it, while we were walking on;
and he, being in a hurry, after he had cut this, to overtake us, unmindfully crossed the path, and steered directly into the woods. The other one that was next to
me, observing his companion was not with us, was alarmed, saying he was subject to fainting fits, and thought he
must have fainted. I immediately threw off my load and
ran back to where I supposed we left him; there I hollo-
ed as loud as my lungs would admit, a number of times.
He at length heard, and stopped. He was completely
lost, and could not find his way back. He answered, and
I went to him, and put him in the right path again.
This frightened me more than all the bears in the woods;
but it however served as a lesson to others, never to give
up a certainty for an uncertainty.

CHAPTER VI.

THE summer of 1823, Chancellor Kent, from New York, came to my house with two young gentlemen. As he was desirous of passing this way, he hired a private conveyance here, after leaving the stage, which did not then pass through the Notch, as the mail was then sometimes transported on horseback and sometimes in a one horse wagon. He chartered me to carry them to Conway, when they would take the stage again. After putting up with our accommodations through the night, in the morning I harnessed my two mares, who had each a young colt, and they took the road forward and their mothers behind, which made a regular team; this amused them much. I carried them to the destined place, the same day; and while on the way, we had an interesting time in exchanging jokes, etc.

In July, another man and myself took blankets, provisions, and other necessary things, for a small party, who were going to stay the second night on Mount Washington, as they were desirous of being there and seeing the appearance of the sun, when it should set in the evening and rise in the morning. After staying at the foot of the hill over night, we ascended, and being there in season, went to work and built three stone cabins. We then collected a quantity of dry moss, laid it in them for beds, spread our blankets, and at an early hour, on this elevated spot, retired to rest, now prostrate

on the ground, so much nearer Heaven than what we had
ever been accustomed. Our sleep was not exactly sound,
but was interrupted by dreams, which one would naturally suppose would be the case. In the morning we awoke
betimes to view the object we came for. We had the
advantage of our neighbors in seeing the appearance of
light first; and when the sun rose, it came up, as it were,
behind a veil, and appeared the bigness of a good sized
cart-wheel. We could look upon it without straining
our eyes, as well as we can look upon the full moon; and
then it rose from behind this cloud, and came out in its
full splendor and glory. This was the first night I ever
slept on Mount Washington. One of the party made the
following lines :

> The Muses' most inspiring draught,
> From Helicon's pure fountain quaff'd,
> What is it, to the rising sun,
> Seen from the top of Washington!
> Canst thou bear a dreary night?
> Stranger! go enjoy the sight.

We then returned over Munroe, Franklin and Pleasant
Mountains, following our old path, came in at the Notch,
and from there home.

It was now beginning to be fashionable for ladies, attended by gentlemen, to visit this place, both for health
and amusement, and we were most of the time crowded.
As our house was so small, we could accommodate but
a few at a time, although we could give them clean beds;
but they were obliged to stow closely at night, and near
the roof, as we had but two small sleeping rooms down
stairs, and these were generally occupied by ladies; the

gentlemen were under the necessity of going up stairs, and there lay so near each other, that their beds nearly touched; but as we did all we could for them, they seemed satisfied with it.

In August, there came at one time, three different parties, which made quite a number for us in those days. Early in the morning, the gentlemen set out for the hills, leaving the ladies to amuse themselves and achieve such victories as they, in their capacity, might think proper. After dinner, the ladies inquired if the hill north of my house had ever been visited, and whether there were any views that were interesting? And after receiving an answer in the affirmative, they started and took the nearest route, which was a very rough one. One of them being active and ambitious, said she would be the first one up. She then set out in great haste, supposing that this could be done in a few minutes. The day being warm, she soon grew fatigued, and perspiring freely, she gave out before she had attained half its summit, and returned nearly exhausted. She said this hill should bear the name of Mount Deception, for its deceptive appearance; and, from this circumstance, it has since been called by that name. The other ladies, taking it with more moderation, reached the top of the hill; here they could see some habitations in Bethel, and had a good prospect of the valley, and the way in which we travel to go up the mountain, which is a delightful view. They returned in a different way. In the evening I amused them with the sound of my long tin horn, sent me by a gentleman from Portland, for the benefit of the echo, which, when the horn was sounded, would vibrate along the side of the hill, until the sound would die away on the ear. This had a strange effect on one lady, as she said it seemed when the horn was sounded as if it were answered by a supernatural voice from Heaven, inspiring her with strange ideas or feelings, which she never before experienced.

Again, we had another party come, from which I will relate a circumstance. We went up the mountain, the weather then looking favorable, until we reached the top of the hill, and then we went into a cloud, which was dark all around us. Having reached the summit, and not having any landmarks to direct us back, and not being acquainted with the weather here, we staid only long enough for them to carve their names, and then tried to return; but I was lost, myself, for a short time. I started toward the east, and we wandered about until we came near the edge of a great gulf. Here we staid and amused ourselves by rolling such large stones as we could find loose, and these being started, went with such force that they would take others with them, and then rest only in the valley beneath. Although a little danger was encountered in this kind of sport, had one of us slipped accidentally and been precipitated down the gulf, yet it was actually a grand sight; and while we were enjoying this, there came up a strong wind and carried away the clouds in as short time as they had been gathering and coming on. Now what a contrast, to have the darkness all taken away, and then a perfect, clear sunshine come on. It cheered all hearts. We then had a good prospect of all the country around, and this opportunity was not lost. We could see what course to steer, beat our way toward the path, and succeeded in finding it, and returned home.

At another time I went up the mountains with two gentlemen. We started in the morning, with the prospect of a clear day, and having attained the summit, could see the clouds gathering below us; and as the lightning streaked along in the clouds, a rumbling noise was heard, but not like the sound of thunder. Here, as there was nothing to give it an echo, it only sounded like a rumbling noise in the distance, but it was near us. What a situation to be placed in, so high in the air! Like the eagle, we could now look down upon a raging storm, while the atmosphere above was perfectly clear. We then went down to Blue Pond, and, while here, the wind came up, attended with hail, which descended with such violence that it seemed as though every hail stone left a mark on our faces; and to prevent losing our hats, we were obliged to tie them on with our handkerchiefs. We went struggling against the wind a distance of one and a half miles; sometimes it was with difficulty we could stand or walk, until after we had attained this distance; we then got below the wind, and could now pursue our way home, in a moderate rain. We arrived there completely drenched.

Two gentlemen from Boston came, and went up the mountain. After remaining on its summit as long as they wished, returned by the way of Blue Pond, and from thence down Escape Glen, as they termed it, to the camp,—a passage romantic, but precipitous, where one of them, as they said, came near losing his life, by taking hold of an old root of a tree to support himself, which gave way. He was over a perpendicular precipice of fifty feet, but fortunately saved himself, and returned safely home. He experienced no injury, save that of being frightened.

This spring and summer, the gray cat or Siberia lynx, troubled us very much, making several depredations among our sheep and geese, and we underwent some fears for the safety of our children. These cats were bold and not afraid of man, never putting themselves much out of the way to shun him. At one time a gentleman was coming down Cherry Mountain in a sleigh, and saw two of these animals engaged in a quarrel, as it appeared to him, in the road before him ; and it was with some difficulty that he could convince them that the road belonged to him ; but with some entreaties, they separated, one on either side, giving him just room to pass. He said he might have reached them with his whip, but as they were content to let him pass, he was content not to disturb them in their angry looking position. I set traps, and in various ways tried to catch them. I even killed a hen and set her for bait, feathers and all on, in the appearance of life, supposing they would like this, but they only seemed to amuse themselves by this, in coming up and looking at it, and then passing on. At length I thought of one more thing to try. I took some pickled fish, which had a strong smell to it, for bait ; and the first one afterward who happened this way, had the curiosity to see what was there ; and as the trap was between him and the fish, he put his foot in the trap and was held fast. He managed to move the trap a little distance, but was soon fastened by the grapple, which caught in a thicket, where I found him. He was lying partly hid, and I did not perceive him until I came near stepping upon him, when he suddenly started up, and I as soon sprang back to find something to defend myself with; and when prepared, entered into an engagement with him, which was rather a tough one, he having the advantage, being in the thicket. I conquered him at last, and brought him home in triumph; he measured six feet and over. In this, and similar ways, I caught six of them. The next spring I took one by stratagem, as I was traveling down through the Notch with a team and dog. Below the Notch House, while we were going on, my dog came upon the track of one of these animals, who had just crossed the road before us; the dog followed so closely that the animal sprang into a tree, and then the dog sat at the bottom, barking earnestly at him. I knew he had something, and leaving my team in the road, took my small axe with me, which I always carried, and went to him; he was up a tree thirty feet, watching the movements of the dog. I then cut two birch sticks, the longest I could select, and twisting the ends put them together, and at one extremity of the stick I made a ring with a slip noose to it; this I ran up through the boughs of the tree, and so managed to get it over his head, then giving a sudden jerk, brought him down ten feet; he caught on a limb, and the halter slipped off. I then fixed it again, and he being nearer, gave me a better chance. I put it over his head, down on his neck, so that it held him fast, and then giving another jerk, fetched him to the ground. The dog instantly seized him, but the cat soon extricated himself by tearing him with his claws, which he seemed to know how to apply very actively, causing the dog to cry for quarter. The cat then gave a jump the length of the stick, over a spruce top four feet high, with the halter still around his neck, and here he hung; I then fell to beating him with a club, which I had previously prepared, and the dog, recovering himself, assisted me, and we soon finished him. Shouldering my booty, I returned to my team, and placing him on it, carried him down to my father's, and there leaving him, resumed my journey. On my return I took him home. I never saw but one afterward, and that, as I was coming down Cherry Mountain; the dog drove him into a tree, and I followed him up there, myself; but the trees were so thick that he jumped from one to another, and thus made his escape, for the time. But shortly after, I had a trap set in a brook, near the mouth, where it empties into the Amanoosuc, hoping that I might catch an otter; the trap set near the end of a log which crossed the stream, and was fastened by a chain to a limb, six feet above the water, and this cat, wanting to cross the brook here, walked on the log, when, stepping off, he put his foot in the trap, and there he was held. He managed to get back on the log, and then on the limb, and wound up the chain in such a manner, that he could not get either way; here I found him, dead, suspended between heaven and earth. On these animals I had a premium of three dollars apiece, which nearly paid me for my loss and trouble. After making this havoc among them, I was never troubled with any of them again, while living at the Hills, and there being no signs of them, I supposed I destroyed the whole family.

In October there came to my house, a family from Portsmouth, who had hired a man to carry them to Jefferson in a coach, and it had begun to snow before they arrived here, and they concluded to put up with me for the night, and had it not been for this circumstance, they would have had time to have finished their journey that night. The next morning, as it continued to snow, the man hired me to carry them the rest of the way, and the other returned home. They staid the next day, and the second morning, as it had done snowing, I harnessed up two horses, and put them on before a good yoke of oxen, and commenced my task; and when going over Cherry Mountain, the snow was plumb two feet deep. We worked hard all day to get twelve miles; there I staid over night, and the next day I made out to get home again. This snow all went off before winter.

I had this fall engaged the Notch House, and agreed to furnish it with such things as are necessary for the comfort of travelers and their horses. It is the case sometimes in the winter, that if no one lived here, people, it seems, must suffer with the cold, for the wind comes down through the narrows of the Notch with such violence, that it requires two men to hold one man's hair on, as I have heard them say. I have never found it to blow so hard here as to equal this, yet it has blown so hard as to take loaded sleighs and carry them several rods to a stone wall, which was frozen down so firmly that it was impenetrable, and there the sleigh stopped. I heard a second-hand story from a clergyman, that the wind was once known to blow so hard here, that it took a log chain and carried it to the distance of a mile or more; but I do not tell this as a fact, only as a story which is told, and perhaps believed by some credulous folks who live at a distance and form strange ideas of this place. At one time I was going down to the Notch House with a load of hay, to an occupant there, when going round the elbow of the Notch there came a gust of wind and upset my load toward the gulf; I instantly turned myself, and placed my feet against the railing on the road, that was put there for the purpose of keeping horses from running off, which, if I had not done, my load must have gone over a precipice of a hundred feet, with the horses attached to it, and I cannot say where I should have been.

Here I waited until the wind abated, and then I put my shoulder under and righted it again, and went on. At another time some young people were going down here, and at or near the top of a long hill, one of the company's horses made a misstep and fell. In the fall, by some means or other, the horse entirely cleared himself of all his harness, and lay by the side of the road, while they were permitted to pass by and go a considerable distance by themselves, and the horse stopped yet behind, which made sport enough for the rest of the company for some time.

The winter of 1824 I bought hay at Jefferson, and carried it sixteen miles to furnish the Notch place with; and I had been advised by my friends to build an addition to my house, which I was at first rather unwilling to do, owing to my limited circumstances not yet being extricated from my first obligations; however, I commenced drawing lumber from Bethlehem, a distance of twelve

miles, and this work, with drawing hay and other necessary business, occupied my whole time for this winter.
In the spring I hired hands, and went industriously to
work, and soon had a frame thirty-six by forty feet, two
stories high, and it was raised by thirteen hands. This
was thought to be sufficiently large to accommodate all
who would be likely to call upon us. During the summer
and fall we had the outside finished and painted. In
July, we had a number of excellent gentlemen, some of
whom were from the Southern States, to visit us, who
gave us an account of their manner of living there, and a
description of the country, manners, etc., which was interesting; and another gentleman, a painter, from a different part of the country, who took some beautiful
sketches of the hills and likewise of the Notch, which
sketches, I presume, have been finished and presented to
the public.

In August, we had another party who ascended the
mountain, and while there the clouds passed swiftly from
under us and a rumbling noise of thunder was heard,
which excited a clergyman, one of the party, who offered
up a very appropriate prayer to Almighty God, and then
we sung Old Hundred, in the lines set to that tune.

CHAPTER VII.

THIS summer, owing to the dampness of the place on Mount Washington, where we built stone cabins, we never but once afterward slept in them. I went to Portland and there bought a marquee, for which I paid twenty-two dollars, sufficiently large for eighteen persons to sleep under at a time; and a sheet iron stove, for which I paid six dollars; and these I carried on or near the top, spreading our tent near a spring of water which lives here. Our tent with the tackling belonging to it, I had put up in as small a compass as possible, and it weighed eighty pounds and over. I then took it on my back and carried it almost the whole distance myself; but I had some visitors then going up with me, and one who looked and thought he felt as stout as I was, kindly offering to assist and relieve me, took my load, but could not carry it far before he was satisfied with it. He then laid it down and I took it again and conveyed it the remainder of the way; and on the way we cut a pole to stretch this round, and I carried that up also. This, however, did not last long, as the storms and wind are so violent here that we could not keep it in its place, and it soon wore out. At the same time we carried up a piece of sheet lead which I had purchased, eight or ten feet in length, seven inches wide, and the thickness of pasteboard; this was put round a roller, which I made for the purpose, for the benefit of those who went up and wished to leave their names, which they could now do much quicker and easier, with an iron pencil which I made, than they could carve them with a chisel and hammer on a rock.

Shortly after this, a gentleman from Boston came and went up the hill without a guide, and while on the summit of this majestic mountain, he thought it a favorable occasion to reconsider the doings of the meeting held at the same place on the 27th day of July last, by Thomas C. Upham and others. He called a meeting for the purpose, and as no other prominent personage seemed to offer, he was invited to take the chair, *nemine contradicte*. He fully explained the object of the meeting, to wit : To select a suitable man to govern this mighty people. He soon heard the name of the Hon. Jas. Kent, late Chancellor of New York, called out from all parts of this immense canopy, under which our meeting was held. On taking the vote, it was unanimously agreed to recommend him as a candidate to fill the highest office in this republic. When he declared this vote, applause, long and loud, rent the sky, the echo of which still fills his ears. Believing the above nomination will be hailed with joy by those who wish a *virtuous man*, unused to intrigue, to rule over us, and who are *heart-sick* of cabal, political juggling and roguery, he hereby published it to the nation, believing it his duty so to do. He then returned home well satisfied with the proceedings of the day ; an account of which he published in the Album and left. I have here transcribed it, to show how many different objects are sought on these mountains.

September 10, another party ascended the mountain ;

the day was clear and warm; they found ice in great quantities, from four to six inches thick.

October 2, Captain Partridge came with fifty-two Cadets, and as I was gone from home, Lucy managed and got along with them as well as she could. It was not far from the middle of the day when they arrived, and the Captain, as he had been there before, took a part of them and proceeded toward the camp that night, for the purpose of having the next day before him to make some barometrical observations, and the others went the same afternoon down to view the Notch and its wonders. Thence they returned the same evening and staid with us that night. Lucy gave them all the beds she then had, which was not enough to accommodate them. Some slept on the floor, and some slept in the barn, and at one time a number stacked themselves up in a pile by the side of the fence, in the bright moonshine; but this was not a very comfortable situation, for the bottom ones removed their quarters and returned to the barn. The next morning after breakfast, they took a guide and went and met the Captain and his party coming down the hill; they, however, went up, and back as far as the camp, and there staid that night, while the former party came home, and the next morning they all came together again to breakfast. We had one room half the bigness of the house, which we used as a kitchen, a victualing room, a sitting room, and when crowded, a sleeping room; but we were a little better off at this time, having a cooking stove in a woodshed adjoining the house, but this place was not large enough to do all the work in, therefore we had to use the kitchen to do the rest of the work in.

4

Though suffering all these inconveniences, Lucy never murmured or complained, but bore them with patience, saying there was an overruling Providence in all these things, and that these and some other difficulties were to try us, and she would always put some good construction on everything, and view things on the bright side, and in this way we got along, and lived peaceably together without any difficulty.

In the winter of 1825, I bought brick for a chimney, and had to draw them twenty-one miles, which made quite a job of it; the lumber I had to draw from twelve to twenty miles. This, with what other work I had to do, made a good winter's work for me. The doors we had made in the winter, and in the spring the joiner came and finished his work; and then, the mason and painter completed the rest, so that we had a house for our summer company, which increased yearly.

At this time we began to feel quite comfortable, as we had plenty of house room. This room required a good deal of furniture to make it any way decent, without extravagance, and we were obliged to buy such things as were really necessary, which did not seem much like getting out of debt, but still plunging in deeper and deeper. Yet my creditors were so generous as seldom or ever to call upon me, when I was unprepared to meet them.

The first day of June, some gentlemen came, and went up the mountains. They had rather a fatiguing time of it, as we had not cleared the path of windfalls, which had fallen the preceding winter, and it was excessively warm in the woods, the thermometer standing at 95 deg., and on the summit at 60 deg. Heat so excessive is seldom experienced here. Notwithstanding, however, the extreme labor which we had to encounter, we felt ourselves amply rewarded by the clouds which enveloped the summit. The clouds on the top, occasionally broke away and gave us beautiful views; others appearing between the mountains around us, now rolling up their sides, and now descending into the valley beneath, forming a magnificent prospect. As I have made some extracts from the visitor's album, I will make a few more, to show the difference of the weather, and the different descriptions given by them, as they come in course, not all, but only those which I think will be interesting for those who have never been here, so that they can form some idea of the place.

July 12th, two gentlemen and a small boy came, and ascended the hill, unattended by a guide; they went within three quarters of a mile of the top, when they were overtaken by a thunder storm. One of them, with the boy, returned to the camp, while the other persevered and reached the summit. Mr. Hibbard, one of the gentlemen spoken of, gives the following account of his ascension :—" In the aforesaid excursion, I, the said Hibbard, with precipitancy, ascended the mountain, and reached the summit within three or four hundred feet, when I was overtaken with a thick cloudy vapor, which rushed on with awful majesty, unmolested in its course even by the mountain itself, and so completely beclouded my way that it was with difficulty I reached the summit. I then concluded to descend to the camp, but was met by the cloud, which shot forth vivid lightning all around me. It was then dark, and I made my way for the tent, on the summit; and made myself as comfortable as I could through the night, but suffered some with cold." The following lines were afterward appended by M. F. M. Waterford jr.:

"Whoe'er thou art, go view the White Mountains,
  Their cloud cap't tops and crystal fountains;
  Ascend and breathe the healthy mountain air,
  And view the prospect spread so wide and fair—
  Then view the Notch, my friend, return and tell,
  Could you have spent your time and cash so well?"

The evening before, the view was grand and sublime. The same afternoon, a party from the Columbian Academy, with their instructor, Rev. S. R. Hall, came, and at six o'clock in the evening set out, intending to reach the camp that night, but they were overtaken by the storm before mentioned; and I make use of their language to describe it. "The members of the Columbian Academy, proceeded at a very late hour, six o'clock, P.M., from E. A. Crawford's, and were overtaken with a severe thunder shower, before we arrived at the first camp three miles distant, and there was darkness *impenetrable.* We were obliged to camp in an old camp, wet, cold and uncomfortable, but we took no cold; started at three o'clock, and arrived at the other camp, where we obtained fire, and soon had a comfortable breakfast. We then went toward the top of Mount Washington, and found it covered with impenetrable fog and clouds. We returned pleased but disappointed."

July 27th, four gentlemen came from different parts of the country, and I went with them on their excursion.

We started, and staid over night at the camp; early the next morning we went up Mount Washington and there enjoyed a noble prospect. On our way home, two of them and myself determined to fish, and after we had arrived at the right place, we turned out and went to the river, while the other two proceeded toward home. Here we commenced our work, and as fast as we could put in a hook, the trout caught it. One of the party had three hooks attached to his line, and frequently caught three at a time; but the bushes were so thick here, that they would get tangled and pester him. I told him I could beat him in taking them; for I could put in and take one at a time, and get them faster than he could. He came to the same conclusion, and accordingly took off all his hooks but one. We had sport enough until satisfied I could carry no more home, and then we left off. We caught in a short time one hundred and thirty-five trout, as many as I could stow in my provision sack, then went home, with a plenty of this kind of food to last during their stay, which was enjoyed with equal pleasure, as when we were taking them.

About this time a botanist came, who was making a collection of the plants of the White Mountains, as he could obtain here some rare ones, such as are not to be found elsewhere in America. I accompanied him in some of his tours around the mountains, and learned the different plants and names, and the different places where they grew. He went three times up and around the hills, and staid some weeks with us. In one of his excursions, he was accompanied by three gentlemen and a guide; and the following description of the excursion

was given by one of the party: "Left Mr. Crawford's
house at seven o'clock, A.M., and reached the summit at
one o'clock, P.M. In the afternoon we were governed by
the botanist and his guide. We concluded to camp on
the summit, and accordingly stowed ourselves away upon the moss on the lee side of a rock, without fire or candles, shivering and shaking in the mountain breeze, like
aspen leaves freezing with cold, the thermometer standing, at sunrise, at 38 degrees. In the morning, two of
them descended to the camp, while the botanist, in company with the other, coasted along by Blue Pond and
Mount Munroe, and descended the mountain by the
most villainous break-neck route of the Amanoosuc. God
help the poor wight who attempts that route, as we did.
And now, gentle reader, Heaven bless you and preserve
your goings forth forevermore. Good day." On the
4th of July, 1825, I think it was, but I may be mistaken
in the exact time, although I was not concerned in the
affair which then took place, a party from Jackson came
up, on the other side of the Hills, and after enjoying the
prospect as much as they chose, and using the spirit
which we had left there in bottles,—which I justified
them in doing, but did not justify them in carrying away
the bottles, which belonged to mother,—robbed the hills
of the brass plate, my sheet lead and everything left
there by our friends, carrying all away. The lead, I was
told, was run into balls; the bottles, of course, were useful; but what use they could make of the brass, with the
Latin inscription thereon, I am not able to say. But one
thing I know, it discovered a thievish disposition to take
things which did not belong to them, and could not do

them any good, things which had been placed there with care, and was expected to remain, and would undoubtedly have remained but for these mischievous persons, who did not understand what belonged to good manners. I have felt myself condemned for not prosecuting them, as they ought to have been chastised and dealt with in a manner according to their deserts. They were found out, and promised to return the things they had purloined; and that was all they ever did about it; but the names are known, and their deeds are registered.

In August, a gentleman came from Boston, attended by his sister. She had made every suitable preparation before leaving home, and was determined to ascend the mountain, although she had been tried to be discouraged on her way, by all who knew her intentions, yet she was not so easily turned, she did not mean that there should be anything lacking in a good will. She desired Mrs. Crawford to go with her, and as she had been, for a long time, anxious to go, I consented; and in the afternoon, having everything in readiness at four o'clock, we started. We rode to the woods, and, each taking a cane, pursued our journey. We walked that night nearly six miles, and arrived at the camp in good season, with a tolerable prospect for the next day. Here all spent the night well, and early in the morning left for the mountain, but before we had got up fairly out of the woods, there came on a fog, with a thick mist of rain; this was a great disappointment to us. A council was held, and we agreed to return to the camp, and there wait for another day. We accordingly descended to the camp, and spent the remainder of the day; in the night it all cleared away, and the next morning, in good season, we were on the summit. How delightful! Now the sun had risen, and as the rain had laid the smoke, the air was perfectly clear and warm, not a cloud nor a vapor to be seen. We could look in every direction and view the works of nature as they lay spread before us; could see towns and villages in the distance, and so clear was the atmosphere, that we could distinguish one house from another; but should I attempt to describe the scenery, my pen would fail for want of language to express my ideas of the grandeur of the place. The butterfly was here, busily employed like ourselves, but, perhaps, not in the same way. I have here seen, seemingly, being a mile in the air and a mile above vegetation, squirrels and mice, near the top of this hill, and large flocks of ravens, ducks, pigeons, robins and various other birds, fly over and around; a flying squirrel was once caught here, and also a rabbit; partridges are found in the vicinity, and insects of various kinds. · After staying a sufficient length of time, we all started for home. Mrs. Crawford went and returned without any assistance, excepting in descending what is called Jacob's Ladder, where I assisted her a short distance. We arrived at the camp, and taking some refreshment, proceeded home, where we arrived about six o'clock. The ladies considered themselves richly paid for their trouble and fatigue, walking nearly eighteen miles. This was the second party of ladies which ascended the mountains; never after this did we persuade ladies to follow their example, but discouraged them whenever we could, endeavoring to prevent them from attempting it, as we thought it too much of an undertaking; but when they became decided and must go, we did all we could to assist them.

The appended extract gives a description of the tour: "The weather was tolerably clear, many clouds floating about, but not so as to obscure the sun. The wind blowing keen and very strong, prevented our stay longer than half an hour, on the top. The view, of course, is very extensive, and presents a great sameness on every side; barren and bleak, innumerable hills, many ponds, and the Green Mountains may be discerned in the more distant view. The river Amanoosuc presents one of the most pleasing objects, in its descent from Blue Pond, forming a sheet of silver down the mountain, and winding its serpentined course in the valley. This, contrasted with the deep shade of the pines and other trees, in some degree, relieves the eye. Several small streams uniting their waters with this river, soon make a sufficient body for trout fishing, many trout of a small size being caught in it. The weather improved on our descent, and after amusing ourselves to our notice, we returned about six o'clock, took supper and again rested all night in the camp, and the next morning arrived at Mr. Crawford's to breakfast."

I will omit making any more extracts, but will insert fragments of the remaining album, (much being lost,) and return to what transpired at home, according to my own knowledge. The following is transcribed from the album, being written there in the handwriting of Dr. Park : "August 27, 1825, John Park, Mrs. Park, Louisa Jane Park, John C. Park and Mary Ann Park, of Boston, Mass., arrived at Mr. Crawford's, with the intention

4*

of ascending Mount Washington. Unfortunately for us,
Mr. Crawford had left home a few hours before we arrived, for Lancaster, and was not expected to return until the evening of the next day. Being limited as to
time, and the mountains appearing clear, except a little
bluish smoke, we determined to proceed on our visit. On
the 28th, at two o'clock P.M., we set out, with a young
man for our guide, (Mr. William Howe); took the carriage down to the field about a mile and a half from the
house, where we were to enter the woods.

"In justice to Mrs. Crawford, I must here mention, that
beside all her civilities, she added the very friendly offer to attend the ladies to the top of the mountain, and
expressed the most kind anxiety for them. After a walk,
not very fatiguing, and, to us, in many parts, romantic
and pleasant, we arrived at the camp twenty minutes before seven. Here Mr. Howe made us a roaring fire, prepared us supper, and all of us, sachems and squaws, be-
took ourselves to the apartment alloted to us. About
midnight it began to rain furiously, but as the clouds
came from the west we were still in hopes of a clear day.
In the morning clouds flying thick, but as blue sky was
occasionally visible, we concluded to ascend, and, after
breakfast, took our departure from the camp, ten minutes
past seven, on the morning of the 29th. Hitherto the
path had been on a general but moderate ascent. The
camp is on the Amanoosuc, and on quitting it, we began
immediately to ascend the steep, here making an angle of
45 degrees. To be particular would be tedious. The task
is excessively laborious; for ladies, though not impractic-
able, it is too severe. Having been joined at the camp

by our driver, Batchelder, each lady had an assistant, and though after passing the woods and bushy region, the wind became very fresh, we all continued to ascend, scrambling over the cliffs for some time. At last, exhausted by fatigue, and coming to a shelf of rocks which appeared more than usual steep and difficult, Mrs. Park and my daughter Mary Ann, concluded it impossible to proceed. Unpleasant as it was to separate so near the summit, for we were now within three quarters of a mile from the apex, we saw no other plan; and, lodging Mrs. Park and Mary Ann in a cleft between large rocks, where they would be in some degree sheltered from the wind, we proceeded, my daughter Louisa Jane, having Mr. Howe to support her on one side and Batchelder on the other. It was a desperate business; the wind grew more violent every step we ascended, and the fog or cloud which enveloped us was wet as rain. At twenty-five minutes past ten, we reached the top, in the midst of a dismal hurricane—no prospect—but certainly our situation partook much of the sublime, from our known elevation, the desolation around us and the horrors of the tempest.

"I have experienced gales in the Gulf Stream, tempests off Cape Hatteras, tornadoes in the West Indies, and been surrounded by water spouts in the Gulf of Mexico, but I never saw anything more furious or more dreadful than this. I staid on the top but five minutes, anxious for those whom we had left. In less than half of an hour, I found them safe, though cold and anxious. The rest of our party soon arrived, and taking a little refreshment, we began to descend together. Soon after we left the regions of barrenness and desolation and entered the woods, we were met by Mr. Crawford himself, who had kindly come out to see what might be our situation. We arrived safe and well at the encampment, at fifteen minutes after one, took a little refreshment, and continued our return to Mr. Crawford's, where we arrived precisely at six o'clock, P.M., having been absent about twenty-eight hours.

"Gentlemen, there is nothing in the ascent of Mount Washington that you need dread. Ladies, give up all thoughts of it; but if you are resolved, let the season be mild, consult Mr. Crawford as to the prospects of the weather, and with every precaution, you will still find it, *for you*, a tremendous undertaking.

"Though we were disappointed after all we had read and heard, in not having Mr. Crawford for our guide, yet we had no reason to complain. Mr. Howe, who conducted us, will be found a faithful and obliging young man. Of Mr. and Mrs. Crawford's kindness and attention, during our short stay here, we have ample reason to join in the common report of all travelers."

CHAPTER VIII.

In September, the same year, a small party of gentlemen and three ladies came to visit the mountains, and I went with them. We staid at the camp over night; next day we went up the hill and back again to the camp, with little trouble or fatigue. After this, when walking on a more level way, one of the ladies became lame in her ankles, and it was with difficulty she could walk. I then took off the bundle of clothes from my back and made a good cushion of them, and placed them on my right shoulder, took my hat in my left hand; the gentlemen then sat her upon my right shoulder, and I brought her some miles in this way quite well. I have brought gentlemen along in a similar way, when they thought they could go no further.

The following is another extract from the album: "When we started in the morning, we were fearful of rain, but the weather was good and the temperature of the air comparatively warm on the summit. Our prospect but ill repaid us the fatigue of ascending, as the atmosphere was smoky. After remaining on the summit for more than an hour, and singing Old Hundred, in which the whole party joined, at half past eleven o'clock, we began to descend, and reached the camp in two hours and a half. Here the party rested and refreshed about an hour; left the camp and arrived at Mr. Crawford's at seven o'clock in the evening. As the ladies of our party make a third of the number who have reached the summit of Mount Washington, something may be expected to be said of them and of the practicability of the ascent for ladies. Miss Harriet C. Woodward performed the ascent and descent of the mountain and the walk from the camp to Mr. Crawford's, with much less fatigue than could have been expected. Miss Lawrence suffered a little more. Miss Elizabeth Woodward supported the ascent and descent to the camp tolerably well, but became excessively fatigued and lame during the return walk from the camp to Mr. Crawford's, and had it not been for the kind and humane attention and assistance of Mr. C., which we here record with much gratitude. would scarcely have been able to have reached Mr. C.'s, In conclusion, could ladies be carried and find a little more comfortable accommodations on the mountains, the ascent of Mount Washington even, would be a comparatively easy achievement. As it is, ladies, do not attempt it; at least, *never but in fair weather.* Of Mr. Crawford's kindness and humanity nothing need be said; all who visit the mountain will be satisfied with it."

Getting tired of carrying blankets every time we went up this mountain, and not being able to leave them in safety on account of the mice and squirrels, for they would make holes in them, unless we hung them on a tree, and then they were exposed to the weather, sometime in the forepart of the summer, I bought a sufficient quantity of sheet-iron and made a chest that would hold ten bushels, apparently large enough for the man who carried it to lie down and rest himself in. This we placed at the camp and there made a deposit for all things that might be left there. We had eleven blankets, and cooking utensils for cooking a good warm meal, and would frequently add to the variety, by a dish of trout, which could be caught but a few rods from the camp. These I could cook to a charm, much better than an old experienced cook in a city hotel could,—at least, they tasted much better here than there. I had plenty of good salt pork to cook them with, and that is the very thing that gives them a relish; and fatigue would never fail of giving us good appetites. Afterward I made my tea, and then could drink it in clean fresh-washed cups. I had here every convenience for doing all this work. I was presented with a box of tin-ware of a superior quality, from the before mentioned botanist, containing an apparatus sufficient for a number to eat and drink with together; and on the corner of the iron chest, I would sometimes put birch bark from a tree and spread it as a substitute for a cloth, and in this way I have enjoyed many a good meal with my friends.

We had two camps built and they stood facing each other, and there· was a good fire in the middle. The wood we cut from six to eight feet in length and rolled it together, any way or size we could manage, and when one pile burnt out, we would put another on, and thus kept a good fire through the night. One camp was for ladies and the other for gentlemen. For beds we took a large quantity of spruce and hemlock boughs and laid them down, spread our blankets upon them, and this would make a healthy bed. To secure the ladies, we would make a blanket curtain in front of their camp, and they were entirely by themselves. Now the untiring mosquito would sing to us constantly and every now and then would stop and taste a little.

I never knew a single person that ever took cold from these wild excursions. We frequently received letters from invalids saying their healths were much improved by this visit with us.

Now we were in trouble again, there being a complaint for want of a shed and more stable room. The winter of 1826 was at hand with a great deal to do. After having done other necessary business, I went to hauling boards and shingles from the same short distance of twelve miles only, up through the Notch. My father had put him up a new saw-mill, and I could get boards from there now better than from anywhere else, but it was some trouble to draw them up the Notch hills. Some perhaps think this a heavy job, but when a thing is undertaken in good earnest, it is soon over; so with this job. In the spring I hired men and went to work and soon had timber prepared for a stable sixty feet by forty, and a shed to stand between the old stable and the new one, fifty feet by forty, which accommodated . both stables, and the whole length of these buildings was nearly one hundred and fifty feet, in a straight line, facing the road. The outside of these buildings was nearly finished, when a stop was put to all business in consequence of the great rain, which you will soon find recorded.

In June, as my father with a number of men was at work repairing the turnpike road through the Notch, there came on a heavy rain, and they were obliged to leave their work and retire to the house, then occupied

by the worthy Willey family, and it rained very hard.
While there they saw on the west side of the road a
small movement of rocks and earth coming down the hill,
and it took all before it. They saw, likewise, whole trees
coming down, standing upright, for ten rods together,
before they would tip over,—the whole still moving
slowly on, making its way until it had crossed the road,
and then on a level surface some distance before it
stopped. This grand and awful sight frightened the
timid family very much, and Mrs. Willey proposed to
have the horses harnessed and go to my father's, but the
old gentleman told her not to be alarmed, as he said
they were much safer there than they would be in the
road; for, said he, there may be other difficulties in the
way, like the one just described, or the swollen waters
may have carried away some of the bridges, and they
could not be crossed; and after some reasoning with her
in this way she was pacified and remained safely. The
next day, as the storm had abated, they set about removing the burden from the road, which required much
trouble and labor. This seemed to be a warning and it
appeared so to them. Mr. Willey had looked round and
about the mountains and tried to find out a safer place
than the one they then occupied; and, having satisfied
himself, as he thought, placed a good tight cart-body in
such a manner as would secure them from the weather
in case a similar thing should occur, as visitors had advised them to leave the place, as they were anxious for
their safety; and he, it appeared, was fearful, or he
would not have made this effort. But there is an overruling God who knows all things and causes all things to

happen for the best, although we short-sighted mortals cannot comprehend them. Had they taken the advice of St. Paul and all abode in the ship, they might have been saved; but this was not to be their case,—they were suffered to perish.

August 26th, there came a party from the West to ascend the mountain, but as the wind had been blowing from the south for several days, I advised them not to go that afternoon, but they said their time was limited and they must proceed. Everything necessary for the expedition being put in readiness, we all, like so many good soldiers, with our staves in our hands, set forward at six o'clock and arrived at the camp at ten o'clock; and I with my knife and flint struck fire, which caught in a piece of dry punk, which I carried for that purpose, and from that I could make a large fire. This was the only way we had in those days of obtaining fire. After my performing the duties of a cook and house maid, we sat down in the humble situation of Indians, not having the convenience of chairs, and told stories till the time for rest. The wind still continued to blow from the south. In the morning, about four o'clock, it commenced raining, which prevented their hopes of ascending the mountain that day, and not having provisions for another day, and they being unwilling now to give it up, when they had got so near, a meeting was called and it was unanimously agreed that I should go home and get new supplies and then return to them again. I obeyed their commands, shouldered my empty pack, took my leave of them and returned; but, as the rain was falling so fast, and the mud collected about my feet, my progress was

slow and wearisome. I at length got home, and being
tired and my brother Thomas being there, I desired him
to take my place, which he cheerfully consented to do,
and in a short time, he was laden and set forward; and
when arriving at the camp, the party was holding a council as to what was to be done, for the rain had fallen so
fast and steadily that it had entirely extinguished the
fire. They consulted Thomas upon the matter to know
if they had time to get in. He told them that to remain
there would be very unpleasant, as they must suffer with
the wet and cold, not considering danger, but if they
would go as fast as they could, they might reach the
house. Each taking a little refreshment in his hands,
and having the precaution to take the axe with them, set
off in full speed, and when they came to a swollen stream
which they could not ford, Thomas would, with his axe,
fell a tree for a bridge, and then they would walk over.
They got along tolerably well until they came to a large
branch, which came from the Notch. This was full and
raging, and they had some difficulty to find a tree that
would reach to the opposite bank, but at length succeeded in finding one, and they all got safely over, and
those who could not walk, crawled along, holding on by
the limbs; and when they came to the main stream, the
water had risen and come into the road for several rods,
and when they crossed the bridge it trembled under their
feet. They all arrived in safety about eight o'clock in
the evening, when they were welcomed by two large
fires to dry themselves. Here they took off their wet
garments, and those that had not a change of their own
put on mine and went to bed, while we set up to dry

theirs. At eleven o'clock we had a clearing up shower, and it seemed as though the windows of heaven were opened and the rain came down almost in streams. It did not, however, last long before it all cleared away and became a perfect calm. The next morning we were awakened by our little boy coming into the room, and saying, " Father, the earth is nearly covered with water, and the hogs are swimming for life." I arose immediately and went to their rescue. I waded into the water and pulled away the fence, and they swam to land. What a sight! The sun rose clear; not a cloud nor a vapor was to be seen ; all was still and silent, excepting the rushing sound of the water, as it poured down the hills. The whole interval was covered with water a distance of over two hundred acres of land, to be seen when standing on the little hill which has been named and called Giant's Grave, just back of the stable, where the house used to stand that was burnt. After standing here a short time, I saw the fog arise in different places on the water, and it formed a beautiful sight. The bridge which had so lately been crossed, had come down and taken with it ninety feet of shed which was attached to the barn that escaped the fire in 1818. Fourteen sheep that were under it were drowned, and those which escaped looked as though they had been washed in a mud puddle. The water came within eighteen inches of the door in the house and a strong current was running between the house and stable. It came up under the shed and underneath the new stable, and carried away timber and wood, passed by the west corner of the house and moved a wagon which stood in its course.

Now the safety of my father and of the Willey family occupied our minds, but there was no way to find out their situation. At or near the middle of the day (Tuesday) there came a traveler on foot who was desirous of going down the Notch that night, as he said his business was urgent, and he must, if possible, go through. I told him to be patient, as the water was then falling fast, and as soon as it should fall and I could swim a horse, I would carry him over the river. Owing to the narrowness of the intervals between the mountains here, when it begins to fall it soon drains away, and at four o'clock I mounted a large strong horse, took the traveler on behind, swam the river, and landed him safely on the other side and returned. He made the best of his way down to the Notch house and arrived there just before dark. He found the house deserted by every living creature, excepting the faithful dog, and he was unwilling at first to admit the stranger. He at length became friendly and acquainted. On going to the barn he found it had been touched by an avalanche and fallen in. The two horses that were in it were both killed, and the oxen confined under the broken timber tied in their stalls. These he set at liberty after finding an axe and cutting away the timber; they were lame, but soon got over it. What must have been the feelings of this lonely traveler while occupying this deserted house, finding doors opened and bed and clothes as though they had been left in a hurry, bible open and lying on the table as if it had lately been read? He went round the house, and prepared for himself a supper, and partook of it alone, except the company of the dog, who seemed hungry like himself; then quietly lay down in one of these open deserted beds, and consoled himself by thinking the family had made their escape and gone down to my father's. Early the next morning he proceeded on his way and he had some difficulty in getting across some places, as the earth and water were mixed together and made a complete quagmire. He succeeded in getting to father's, but could obtain no information of the unfortunate family. He told this story as he went down through Bartlett and Conway, and the news soon spread.

On Wednesday the waters had subsided so much that we could ford the Amanoosuc river with a horse and wagon, and some of the time limited party agreed to try the ground over again ; so they, with the addition of another small party who came from the West on Tuesday, with Thomas for guide, again set out, while I, with a gentleman from Connecticut, went toward the Notch. After traveling a distance of two miles in a wagon, we were obliged to leave it and take to our feet. We now found the road in some places entirely demolished, and seemingly, on a level surface ; a crossway which had been laid down for many years and firmly covered with dirt,—that to the eye of human reason it would be impossible to move,—taken up, and every log had been disturbed and laid in different directions. On going still a little further, we found a gulf in the middle of the road, in some places ten feet deep, and twenty rods in length. The rest of the road, my pen would fail should I attempt to describe it ; suffice it to say, I could hardly believe my own eyes, the water having made such destruction. Now, when within a short distance of the house, I found the cows with their bags filled with milk, and from their appearance, they had not been milked for some days. My heart sickened as I thought what had happened to the inmates of the house. We went in and there found no living person, and the house in the situation just described. I was going down to my father's to seek them out, but the gentleman with me would not let me go, for he said he could not find his way back alone, and I must return with him. We set out and arrived home at four o'clock in the afternoon.

I could not be satisfied about the absent family, and again returned, and when I got back to the house found a number of the neighbors had assembled and no information concerning them could be obtained. My feelings were such that I could not remain there during the night, although a younger brother of mine, being one of the company, almost laid violent hands upon me to compel me to stay, fearing some accident might befall me, as I should have to feel my way through the Notch on my hands and knees, for the water had in the narrowest place in the Notch taken out the rocks which had been beat in from the ledge above to make the road, and carried them into the gulf below, and made a hole or gulf twenty feet deep, and it was difficult, if not dangerous, to get through in the night, as all those who visited this scene of desolation will bear testimony to ; but my mind was fixed and unchangeable, and I would not be prevailed on to stay. I started and groped my way home in the dark, where I arrived at ten o'clock in the evening. Here I found that the party from the mountain had arrived; as they had nowhere to stay, they were obliged to come in that night. Now we began to relate our discoveries. They had much difficulty in finding their way, as the water had made as bad work with their path as it had done with the road, in proportion to its length. The water had risen and carried away every particle of the camp and all my furniture there. The party seemed thankful that they, on Monday, had made their escape. What must have been their fortune had they remained there? They must have shared the same fate the Willey family did, or suffered a great deal with fear, wet, cold and hunger, for it would have been impossible for them to have come in until Wednesday, and their provisions must have been all gone, if not lost, on Monday night. It seemed really a providential thing in their being saved. No part of the iron chest was ever found, or anything it contained, excepting a few pieces of blanket that were caught on bushes in different places down the river.

The next morning our friends, with gratitude left us; and we had the same grateful feelings toward them, wishing each other good luck.

The same day (Thursday) before I had time to look about me and learn the situation of my farm, and estimate the loss I had sustained, the friends of the Willey family had come up to the deserted house and sent for me. At first I said I could not go down, but being advised to, I went. When I got there, on seeing the friends of that well-beloved family, and having been acquainted with them for many years, my heart was full and my tongue refused utterance, and I could not for a considerable length of time speak to one of them, and could only express the regard I had for them in pressing their hands and giving full vent to my tears. This was the second time my eyes were wet with tears since grown to manhood. The other time was when my family was in that destitute situation. Diligent search being made for them, and no traces to be found until night, the attention of the people was attracted by the flies, as they were passing and repassing underneath a large pile of floodwood. They now began to haul away the rubbish, and at length found Mr. and Mrs. Willey, Mr. Allen, the hired man, and the youngest child not far distant from each other. These were taken up, broken and mangled, as must naturally be expected, and were placed in coffins. The next day they were interred, on a piece of ground near the house, there to remain until winter. Saturday, the other hired man was found and interred, and on Sunday, the eldest daughter was found, some way from where the others were, across the river; and it was said her countenance was fair and pleasant, not a bruise or a mark was discovered upon her. It was supposed she was drowned. She had only a handkerchief around her waist, supposed to have been put there for some one to lead her by. This girl was not far from twelve years of age. She had acquired a good education, considering her advantages, and she seemed more like a gentleman's daughter, of fashion and affluence, than the daughter of one who had located himself in the midst of the mountains. It is said the earliest flowers are the soonest plucked, and this seems to be the case with this young, interesting family; the rest of the

5

children were not inferior to the eldest, considering their age. In this singular act of Providence, there were nine taken from time into eternity, four adult persons and five children. It should remind us, we who are living, to "be also ready, for in such an hour as ye think not, the Son of Man cometh." It was a providential thing, said Zara Cutler, Esq., who was present afterward, that the house itself was saved, so near came the overwhelming avalanche. The length of the slides are several miles down the side of the mountain. The other three children, one daughter and two sons, have never to this day been found; not even a bone has ever been picked up or discovered. It is supposed they must have been buried deep underneath an avalanche.

Mr. and Mrs. Willey sustained good and respectable characters, and were in good standing among the christians in Conway, where they belonged. They were remarkable for their charities and kindness toward others, and commanded the respect of travelers and all who knew them. Much more could be said in their favor, but it would be superfluous to add. Suffice it to remark that the whole intention of their lives was to live humbly, walk uprightly, deal justly with all, speak evil of none.

There came a large slide down back of the house in a direction to take the house with it, and when within ten or fifteen rods of the house it came against a solid ledge of rock and there stopped and separated, one on either side of the house, taking the stable on one side, and the family on the other, or they might have got to the rendezvous; but there is no certainty which of these divisions overtook them, as they were buried partly by the three slides which had come together eighty rods from the house; the two that separated back of the house here met, and a still larger one had come down in the place where Mr. Willey had hunted out a safe refuge. When the slide was coming down and separating, it had great quantities of timber with it. One log, six feet long and two feet through, still kept its course, and came within three feet of the house, but fortunately it was stopped by coming against a brick, where it rested; the ends of trees were torn up, and looked similar to an old peeled birch broom. The whole valley, which was once covered with beautiful green grass, was now a complete quagmire, exhibiting nothing but ruins of the mountains, heaps of timber, large rocks, sand and gravel. All was dismal and desolate. For a monument, I wrote with a piece of red chalk, on a planed board, this inscription:

THE FAMILY FOUND HERE.

I nailed it to a dead tree, which was standing near the place where they were found; but it has since been taken away by some of the occupants of the house and used for fuel.

But to return to my own affairs at home. Fences mostly gone, farm in some places covered so deeply with sand and gravel that it was ruined, and, on the interval, floodwood was piled in great and immense quantities, in different places all over it. The bridge now lay in pieces all around the meadow, and the shed also; there was a large field of oats, just ready to harvest, from which I think I would have had four or six hundred bushels, which was destroyed; also, some hay in the field. My actual loss at this time was more than one thousand dollars, and truly things looked rather unfavorable. After the fire, we had worked hard and economized closely to live and pay our former dues, in which we made slow progress. As it was necessary for the benefit of the public, to buy so many things, which we could not get along without, I could do but little toward taking up my old notes, but still I must persevere, and keep doing while the day lasted, and I thought no man would be punished for being unfortunate. Therefore, taking these things into consideration, I would still continue to do the best I could and trust the event. My father suffered still more than myself. The best part of his farm was entirely destroyed. A new saw mill which he had just put up, and a great number of logs and boards, were swept away together into the sand; fences on the interval were all gone; twenty-eight sheep were drowned and considerable grain which was in the field was swept away. The water rose on the outside of the house twenty-two inches, and ran through the whole house on the lower floors, and swept out the coals and ashes from the fire place. They had lighted candles which were placed in the windows, and my mother took down a pole which she used as a clothes pole, and stood at a window near the corner of the house, when the current run swift, and would push away the timber and other stuff that came down against the house, to keep it from collecting in a great body, as she thought it might jam up and sweep away the house, for the water was rising fast. And while thus engaged, she was distressed by the cries of the poor bleating and drowning sheep that would pass by in the flood, and seemed to cry for help, but none could be afforded.

My father at this time was from home, and but few of the family were there, so they made the best they could of it. This came on so suddenly and unexpectedly that almost everything in the cellar was ruined, and a part of the wall fell in.

This loss of my father's property, which he had accumulated only by the sweat of his brow, was so great that he will never be likely to regain it. Many suffered more or less who lived on this wild and uncultivated stream, as far as Saco.

We had now a difficulty which seemed almost insurmountable. The road in many places was entirely gone; the bridges, the whole length of the turnpike, excepting two, a distance of seventeen miles, gone; the directors came and looked at it, and found it would take a large sum to repair it. The good people of Portland, however, to encourage us, raised fifteen hundred dollars to help us with; it was put into the hands of Nathan Kinsman, Esq., to see it well laid out. The directors voted to raise an assessment on the shares, to make up the balance; and that, with some other assistance, was divided into jobs and let out, and we all went to work; and, as it was said, the sun shone so short a time in this Notch, that the hardy New Hampshire boys made up their hours by moonlight.

CHAPTER IX.

WE got along much better with this work than we expected. We were favored with good weather, and had a decent sleigh path for the winter. This great and wonderful catastrophe, which happened among the mountains, caused a great many to visit the place that fall. Among others there came two gentlemen for the purpose of going up to the mountain and visiting the slides, to ascertain the qualities of naked mountains, as they were in search of minerals. We found on the west side of Mount Pleasant, the largest slide; it appeared one thousand acres in dimension had slid off and rested in the valley below. We wandered about, looking at the wonderful works of God, until night overtook us, and then on a ridge of the hill, near the Amanoosuc, by the side of a large pile of floodwood, I built a camp, or wigwam, which was sufficiently large for us then. I cut my wood, struck a fire, and we each took our blanket and retired to rest. As might be expected, the night at this season of the year, was long and cold; a thick mist of rain came on, and our quarters being small, they complained of the cold and want of room. I arose, renewed my fire, and spread my blanket on them, and retired, myself, to a thick fir tree, under whose boughs I took shelter, and soon fell asleep; being very tired, and now having plenty of room, and feeling my companions were more comfortable, I slept till morning. When I returned to my companions they were glad to see the light of another day. I have been over and around the mountains in almost every direction with botanists and with mineralogists. I have been up and down all the slides of any magnitude, and have taken pains to find out if there were any minerals of value there, but have never as .yet found any of consequence.

It has been supposed by some that there were valuable mines somewhere about the mountains. I have searched for these also, but found none. I recollect a number of years ago, when quite a boy, some persons had been up on the hills and said they had found a golden treasure, or carbuncle, which they said was under a large shelving rock, and would be difficult to obtain, for they might fall and be dashed to pieces. Moreover, they thought it was guarded by an evil spirit, supposing that it had been placed there by the Indians, and that they had killed one of their number and left him to guard the treasure, which some credulous, superstitious persons believed, and they got my father to engage to go and search for it. Providing themselves with everything necessary for the business and a sufficient number of good men and a minister well qualified to lay the evil spirit, they set out in good earnest and high spirits, anticipating with pleasure how rich they should be in coming home laden with gold; that is, if they should have the good luck to find it. They set out and went up Dry river, and had hard work to find their way through the thickets and over the hills, where they made diligent search for a number of days, with some of the former men spoken of for guides, but they could not find the place again, or anything that seemed to be like it, and worn out with fatigue and disappointment, they returned. Never since, to my knowledge, has any one found that wonderful place again, or been troubled with the mountain spirit.

I have heard it said by the people of Portsmouth, that when children were at play and happened to fall out with each other, the worst punishment they could inflict upon their mates was to wish them up at the White Hills, as that was considered the worst place in the world by them. Perhaps their minds had been affected by the story of Nancy, who perished in the woods in attempting to follow her lover. She had been at work in Jefferson for Colonel Whipple, when the heart of this honest girl was won by a servant of his; as he was going in the fall to Portsmouth, he promised to take her along with him, and after they should arrive there, he would make her his wife. She was honest herself and thought him to be also, and as he had contrived every means to please her in all the domestic concerns in which they were engaged, while under the control of the Colonel, she had entrusted him with her money, which had been paid her for her labor, and went to Lancaster to make preparations for the intended journey. While she was preparing, her lover went away with the Colonel and left her behind. She was immediately informed of his treachery, and was determined to pursue him. There had been a deep snow and there was no road, nothing but spotted trees, beside the tracks of the Colonel and her false lover to follow. When she arrived at Jefferson she was wet with snow which had collected upon her clothes, and was wearied. The men that were there tried to persuade her not to go any further, setting forth the many difficulties she would have to encounter, and likewise the danger she would be exposed to in such an undertaking, through a howling wilderness of thirty miles, without fire or food. All these entreaties did not move her, or alter her determination; for such was her love either for the man upon whom she had placed her affections, or the money she had placed in his hands, that she was inflexible. Having a great opinion of her own ability, in her imagination she thought, as they had only been gone some hours, and would probably go no further than the Notch that night, probably camping there, she might, by traveling all night, overtake them before they started in the morning. In this she was disappointed; they had left before she arrived; but from every appearance the fire had not gone out. It may be inquired how it was known that the fire had not gone out there? When a fire is made in the woods, it is made of very large wood, cut and rolled together, and then left to burn, as was evidently the case here, and there will be brands left at each end of the fire. These brands she had put together, and they burnt out, as the ashes plainly showed for themselves when the men found them. She was tired and worn out with fatigue and hunger, having taken nothing with her to eat on the way. Yet her passion was not abated, and she still persevered, thinking she should overtake them. She went on and got a distance of twenty-two miles, when the men thinking she was in earnest, followed her. When she set off in the afternoon, they thought she would not go far before she would come back, and they waited until late in the evening, expecting every moment

5*

to hear the sound of her footsteps at the door; but in vain did they imagine this. They pressed on and found the fire in the situation just described, which made them think she found fire to warm her benumbed limbs. Here they rested only a short time and then proceeded and found her just after crossing a brook, in a sitting position, with her clothes frozen upon her, having wet them while crossing the brook, and her head was resting on her hand and cane which had been her support through the woods, and she was frozen to death.

This place is near my father's, and has ever since, from that circumstance, borne the name of Nancy's Brook, and Nancy's Hill.

"Now in this volume let me build a tomb
For Nancy, love's sweet victim, in her bloom.
Her tragic end, though awful to relate,
Shows how true love controls a woman's fate !
Oh ! had she early given her heart to God,
Perhaps she had not felt the chastening rod.
But let us trust her sins are all forgiven,
And with her Savior, that she rests in Heaven."

J. C. N. I.

The reader would perhaps like to know what became of her lover. Shortly after hearing of this, his own conscience was smitten and he became frantic and insane, and was put into the hospital, where he in a few months after died in a most horrible condition. This is a true story, as I have heard it told by those who were knowing to the facts, as related in the above statement.

CHAPTER X.

OCTOBER 14th, there came a gentleman from Germany to ascend the mountains. I provided him with a good guide, and they set out early in the morning, knowing they must return that evening, as there was no place for them to stay on their way over night. I waited for their return until nine o'clock in the evening, feeling anxious for them, fearing they might be lost, as there had come down in the flood a large quantity of timber and filled up the path, so that it was difficult finding it, not far from the entrance of the woods. I did not know but they might be lost in this place, as it would be dark before they could arrive there, and well knowing the night must be long, cold and tedious, in their destitute situation, I took a lantern and my long tin horn, mounted a horse and proceeded to the woods, where I alighted and then commenced blowing the horn, which was soon answered by the guide. I took my light and steered toward the sound of his voice; there I found them completely lost, not more than a quarter of a mile from the open ground. When they came there it was dark, and though the guide had been there many times before, and knew the way well, yet the darkness bewildered him so much that it was in vain he tried to get out, and when satisfied he could not, he groped his way about in the dark, and had broken some boughs to lie down upon, without a blanket, and no other cover-

107

ing than the canopy of heaven to cover them. Destitute of food, and not having the means of making a
fire, they had made up their minds to spend the night
in this uncomfortable situation, when the joyful sound
of the horn caught their ears. I soon put them in a way
to get liberated from this place, and when they came to
the horse, I helped the gentleman on his back, and then
we all came home; and a more grateful man than this I
scarce ever saw. When arrived at the house, and finding his situation changed from that cold and lonesome
one to a good warm fire and supper, and the expectation
of a good bed, it almost overcame him.

The winter of 1827 I spent much like the former winter seasons; buying and laying in a still larger share of
provisions than usual, for the benefit of those who
should need them while at work on the road, and for the
purpose of assisting the weary traveler through the deep
snows, and over our rough roads.

In the spring I went to work on my mountain road, as
soon as the ground would permit, and I made a road
suitable for a carriage a distance of one and a half miles
into the woods. We could now ride in a carriage from
my house, three miles, and our custom was at that time,
to carry visitors to the end of the road, and then return
with the carriage, and leave them to try their own
strength from there up and back, and then we would be
ready there on their return, to bring them home again.
I had intended to work on this road every year, when I
could, until I should have completed it to the foot of Mt.
Washington.

After reading the description given by Dr. Park, and

the other party of ladies, shortly after their return, and finding their opinion was that it was not exactly fitting for ladies to attempt such an arduous undertaking, all the ladies that visited the mountain were more willing to give up the idea of the ascent, although they had as much curiosity to view and contemplate things not made with hands; and still they, in general, possess an ambition to excell and attain to such noble and romantic acts, for some energy both of mind and body is required to perform such an enterprise. There had never been but four parties of ladies up the mountain since I had come here to live, now ten years past, and I had promised the ladies that whenever I could make a road suitable for them to ride a part or all of the way to the foot of the hill, I would never, in good weather, discourage them from going there, but would go with them myself, and assist them wherever it was necessary. I had made a road to ride on part of the way, and ladies began to take me at my word, and this summer began to ascend the mountain again. Whenever we had more company than what belonged to any particular party, I would furnish them with another guide, so that they should not be troubled or hindered in the least; they might go with us or by themselves, just as the parties chose. I spent this summer in going up and down the mountain with my friends, visiting the Notch and the desolate Willey House, giving them as good an account of what took place on that memorable night of the second of August last and answering all their inquiries as promptly and correctly as my humble capacity and judgment would allow me to do.

It now became needful for the benefit of the company, as it increased, to have an establishment at the top of the Notch, as many wanted to stop there and leave their horses, and pursue their way down the hill on foot, to view the cascades as they come majestically down the hill and over the rocks, and form such a beautiful silvery sight. The flume, likewise, that is curiously cut out by nature through a solid rock, the avalanches, and then the Willey House, etc. On their return they needed refreshment, and having a disposition to accommodate the public, and feeling a little self-pride to have another Crawford settled here, to make up a road, I consulted with my father, and we agreed to build there and place a brother of mine in the house. We accordingly made a plan upon the best and most convenient construction we could invent, and, in the fall, prepared timber for a frame one hundred and twenty feet in length, and thirty-six feet in width. Just as we were about to raise this, the snow fell so deeply that we were obliged to give it up for the present time.

I think that it was this fall that a man from Falmouth had been to Lancaster and bought some fat sheep and oxen; he had a team of horses and a wagon, and on his way home as he was coming over Cherry Mountain, it began to snow. He arrived at my house, where he put up for the night, and it continued to snow until it had fallen two feet, and over; here he staid until it cleared away, and then he could not travel with his sheep, the snow was so deep. I then, with him, began to contrive means to help him along. We harnessed his horses, and put them to a wagon, the oxen on forward of them;

but this did not make a path sufficient for the
sheep to go in. I then harnessed a horse and drove
a wedge into a short, large, round log, put a chain
around this wedge, and led my horse, and this log
made a complete road for them to go in, single file;
in this way, we got along quite well down into the
Notch, a little way, when the snow became thin, then he
could go without my assistance. I then left my log,
mounted my horse, and returned home, while the traveler pursued his journey, without suffering much inconvenience from the snow. It was no uncommon thing
for us to have two feet of snow, while in Bartlett, they
would not have more than two inches; as we lived so
high in the air, and the mountains generally attract or
hinder the storms, we had snow, while others, who lived
not more than twenty miles distant had rain and sometimes sunshine; such was the variableness of the weather
where we then lived, still in the summer we generally
had a good share of good and clear weather, but spring
and fall were the times when we had most of these
sudden changes. Uncle William says, that in former
days, when they first went there to live, the snow would
sometimes be ten feet deep, and he has seen the time
when they could drive a team of oxen and horses anywhere in the field, on the crust, over stumps and fences,
and draw their wood home from any place they chose,
wherever they could best get it, as this hard crust made
a smooth surface for them to go on. Had it not been
for this, they could not have got along where they did,
because it was rough and stumpy, and from such little
circumstances it seems that there is nothing made in

vain. I have seen the snow so deep when I lived there, that it was difficult for men to pass each other with teams, when they met, until they had stamped down the snow, and made a path for one of them to get out, and then sometimes they would have to unhitch their horses and compel them to turn out, such was the depth of snow; and where there was a crust on it, it was still more difficult. At one time when I was coming home from Portland, with a loaded sleigh, when I got up as far as my father's it was snowing, and there I baited my horses; intending to reach home that night, I went on as far as the Notch House, and there hired a man to help me up the hill, with two horses; we went on part of the way, but the snow was so deep, that his horses would not work and we were obliged to leave the sleigh and return to the house. I had the precaution to put the tongue of the sleigh upward, and the next morning when I came to where I had left the sleigh, all that I could discover of it was the tongue; this stood upright. The rest of it was entirely covered with the snow, and it was then utterly impossible for me to take it with me, so I there left it. A man happened to be with me, who had staid with me the preceding night, and was on his way to Vermont, with an empty single sleigh and a good horse. One of my horses I put on forward of his, and I and the other horse made a track for them to follow; we worked hard half a day to get six miles, such was the quantity of snow that had fallen in a few hours. Other descriptions I could give similar to this, but I do not wish to tire the patience of the reader, with more than what is necessary to show the difference between the climate we live in, and other climates not far from us, and what difficulties and hardships we had to encounter in this region ; but in later years, for some cause, we have not had such quantities of snow, and have not been much troubled with its depth, but many times for the want of it.

In the winter, in the beginning of the year 1828, we went to work and bought lumber, and had it drawn a distance of seventeen and a half miles. I bought my brick, and had to haul them twenty-two miles, which kept us busy through the winter, with what other work we had to do. In the spring we collected men and raised these buildings. I hired two joiners, and they went to work on them.

In June, I again worked on my mountain road, and then made it passable for a carriage, with what I had done the year before, a distance from my house of about six miles, on which I could carry in a wagon, with two stout horses, seven passengers at a time, and this made it much easier for the traveler, for ladies could go up much easier than they could at any other time before. They went oftener, and I spent the most of this summer in ascending the mountain with my friends at the house, and in fishing and hunting with them as much as they chose, and bestowing every act of kindness on them which I was capable of doing. The joiners, with what other assistance we could afford them, had the outside of these buildings finished and the inside so much done that it was comfortable for the winter. We were still at work, when on the 2d day of September we were again visited by a heavy rain, which was as great as tho one we had two years before. The water in some places on the Amanoosuc, where the mountains come near together, was higher than in the former freshet. On the Saco, it was not so high, yet the other freshet had made the channel of the river so wide, that the water flood could pass without being dammed up, or stopped in places, as it had been in the former one, therefore it did not occasion so much damage, but passed majestically along, taking only what lay in its course. The bridges which had so lately been built anew, were mostly taken from their places and moved away, but not so far but that some of them could be brought back and put in their former places again. The road was in many places entirely destroyed. This put an end to all our business, at present, as we did not know what would be the result of this. The joiners packed up their tools and left them and went home. As I was at this time transporting the United States Mail from Conway to Littleton, twice in each week, and it being impossible to go with a horse, we carried it regularly on our backs, without losing more than one single trip, to the satisfaction of our friends and employer. The directors of the turnpike came and looked over the road again, and finding it would take a large sum to repair it and make it passable for the winter, they refused, saying that the corporation was not able then to do it, but must have help from some other quarter and they knew no other way for the Crawfords than that they must remain shut up by them-selves, as they could not then make another road there. This did not exactly correspond with my feelings, to be entirely shut up without any communication with our southern neighbors, and not have the privilege of getting provisions and other necessary things for my family. I concluded I would try my own luck, and see what I could effect myself. I set out in good earnest, took a piece of paper, and a man of judgment with me, and went down through the whole length of the road, and made an estimate of what I thought it would cost to repair it again. I consulted with my father upon the matter, to know what was best to be done, then took my estimate and went down to Portland, and saw where the principal proprietors of the road lived. On my way there I called on one of the directors and took from him a letter directed to one of the principal proprietors and owners, to this purport, that the Crawfords were doing a little on the road, but could not effect much, and we as a corporation, have concluded we cannot do anything, at present, on the road, but must let it remain in the same condition for the winter. After having this letter read, and showing him what I thought it would cost to make it again, this proprietor gave me a power of attorney to act on his shares, and others did likewise, until I had enough to rule the meeting, which it was then my whole business to effect. On my way home, I bought two yoke of oxen, hired men and set them to work on the road. The first Wednesday in October was the time for the annual meeting of the corporation of the turnpike, to adjust their business. When they had transacted their regular affairs, it was put to vote whether there should be an assessment raised to repair the road. There were some against me, but I had the power in my hands and I could rule them as I pleased.

I then, with the advice of my father, voted to raise an assessment on the shares, and that, with what other assistance we had from Vermont, and the adjoining towns around, was sufficient. We divided the broken places into jobs, and let it out to different men to make, similar to the way we had done in former times, and we had a tolerable sleigh path again for the winter. I went to Danville Bank and hired three hundred dollars, to pay off the men, and for other expenses, and, after spending a sum of four hundred dollars more, I was obliged to live without this money for nearly four years, with no interest, and could not get it, until it was collected from the benefit of the road. Such was my reward for persevering and making the road contrary to the opinion of the directors, yet I could not charge them with the fault, for they did not wish to have it done until Congress could assist, or some other means could be devised to help them; but it was done and I did not feel sorry for it, although my prospects suffered; still, as it was for the benefit of the people, and I had done it for the general or public good, I did not mind it so much, as I would have done, had I done it from any selfish motive. But to return to my own affairs at home: a field of grain which was partly cut, and still standing in the shocks, was swept away. As the channel of the river had been made wider in the former flood, it did not bring so much timber as at the other time, yet great quantities of sand and gravel were brought on to my interval, and the bridge and fences upon it were again carried away, and thus my mountain road was again destroyed. My loss of property was then considerable, but I did not make an exact estimate of it at that time,' as there did not seem to be much consolation in counting up one loss upon another. My affairs looked gloomy, and I felt almost discouraged, as one misfortune kept following another, and I could not tell where my troubles would end. But in those times of trouble, Lucy was always calm and unruffled, whenever she thought they proceeded from the hand of God. She received things differently from myself; seldom if ever did she complain for the want of anything, but to know how to bring up our children in the right way, as they then began to be numerous; she would say there was still more work for us to do.

This fall a large number of men were at work on the road down through the Notch, and among them was a young man who was subject to a kind of fits, which would take him suddenly, and sometimes when he was not aware of it. These fits did not hinder him from laboring, though in some measure they affected his mind, and so much so that they always looked after him, and generally kept with or near him, in order that no accident should befall him. At one time he had one of these turns after working hard through the day and at night he was tired; in the evening he showed some signs of wildness, which had been noticed by some of his companions. His father was then with him, but the young man did not wish to sleep with his father that night, but slept with another man. Sometime in the night, as it appears, he was thirsty and wanted some drink; he got up and came down stairs, unnoticed by the rest of the company, went out of doors, and it seemed that he lay down to drink out of a small stream of water which

then crossed the road near the house, and while in the
act of drinking, he was taken with a fit, as it was supposed from every appearance, for in the morning when
the men awoke and came down, and went out· of doors,
they found him, lying dead and stiff, with his face in the
water.   How long he had lain there, they could not tell.
He was taken up and conveyed into the house, where a
rough coffin was prepared for him.   My brother Thomas
being there, came to my house and got a horse and
wagon, and he was carried home, followed by his father,
to Jefferson, the place of his nativity, to his friends and
connections, there to be interred.   Here again we had
an evidence of the uncertainty of life, and the impor-
tance of being prepared to meet death, let it come in
whatever shape it may.   This was a great grief to his
friends for they were in rather low circumstances, and
depended upon him for his labor, to help them support
an aged mother who had been blind for twenty years.
She was the first female settler in Jefferson, and I think
her blindness was caused by a shock from lightning,
which had affected her eyes, and they could not restore
her sight, although some skilful physicians had tried.
She lived to be almost one hundred years old.

I went to Portland and bought furniture for my new
establishment, and supplied it with provisions, and January, 1829, my brother Thomas married and moved in
and took charge of my new stand.   It being a new thing,
and so convenient and accommodating, he had a great
share of the winter company.   It was thought that this
would make a great place of resort for those who would
decline the more arduous undertaking of ascending
Mount Washington, for just behind the house was the

path which we first made to ascend the hills, and a good way might be found, one that could be made fit to ride in, on horseback, by taking a zigzag course from one side of the hill to the other, which would only make the distance a little further, but would make the ascent much easier; and then the eye of the curious might be almost satisfied with the sublime, magnificent and delightful prospect from Mount Pleasant, which is not much inferior in the opinion of some, to that from Mount Washington.

This winter I had given up the transporting of the mail, and I had no great business on hand, beside my necessary employment at home. The 4th of May, grandmother departed this life in the eighty-fourth year of her age, after struggling through several cold winters. Being afflicted with a cough, and worn out with a decline similar to that of consumption, for the cold weather affected her very much, nature at length gave way, and she could withstand it no longer. Our good neighbors and friends assembled and paid their last respects to her remains, and she was interred by the side of her husband on a piece of ground which was selected by them, not far from where they had lived and slept many years of their lives together. Here their bodies will remain until called up at the last day. I have placed some suitable monuments at their graves, which can be plainly seen by their friends, and their inscriptions can be read by all who would like to see and read them.

"Their names and years, spelt by their lettered Muse,
 The place of fame and elegy supply;
And many a holy text around she strews,
 That teach the rustic moralist to die."

In the spring, I gave up the idea, at present, of my carriage road to the mountain, and thought it would answer for a while to make a bridle path to the foot of it. I accordingly went to work and made a path sufficient for a horse to travel in seven miles, and I have sometimes gone further than this, but not often. On arriving at the place, we would alight from our horses and take off our saddles, lay them away, tie the horses to a tree, and thus compel them to remain there until our return, without food generally, with the exception of one whose age and fidelity commanded more attention than the rest, and which at the advanced age of thirty had the spirit of a colt, and would carry a visitor safely and in good style. For him I used to carry, or cause to be carried, a sack of oats, as often as possible; yet this was not exactly the right way of treating the dumb beasts, to ride them on the run, early in the morning the distance of seven miles, and then in a state of perspiration, give them grain immediately, but there was no alternative. It had to be done in this way or not at all, and thus we drilled our horses from day to day, and frequently they have gone on the same route six days in a week. It was wearing to the flesh and trying to the spirits, to stand all day tied to a tree, and then run home again as fast as possible, at night. The only time they had to eat, was a few hours designed for rest, but in this way we traveled the rest of the time while I staid at the mountains, but not without remorse of conscience on my part, as our treatment of the dumb beasts was rather inhuman. But I was not able to remedy it, although I often promised so to do, by carrying in the winter on the snow a quantity of hay for them to eat when we were gone.

This summer there came some botanists from Boston for the purpose of making a collection of plants for themselves, and to collect an assortment to send to Europe, and to get some live ones to send to New York to a friend, to be placed in a botanical garden. I went with them and two other men beside, to assist them in carrying blankets and buffalo skins to make them comfortable during the night, and also other things needful for such an expedition of three days. We traveled over and around the hill; and I and one of them went down into a great gulf, and here we found plenty of snow. One place, I think was worthy of notice, where two ledges of perpendicular rocks stood within six or eight yards of each other, and the snow had drifted over on top of these ledges and covered them both, making a complete roof. The sun had softened this snow by day, but at night it would freeze; this had been done so many times in succession that it had formed a crust which was almost impenetrable; and I could not safely walk upon it, because it was glassy and slippery, and I could not make a dent upon it with the heel of my boot; and underneath this the ground was filled with water, and warm springs seemed to be there, which had caused the snow to melt away from under. Such was the size of this empty space that a coach with six horses attached, might have been driven into it. I do not know how far this cavern extended, as I did not go far into it, for the water was fast dropping from the roof, but it appeared to be of considerable length. It was a very hot day, and not far from this place, the little delicate mountain flowers were in bloom, and here we procured as many as we chose.

6

There seemed to be a contrast,—snow in great quantities and flowers just by,—which wonderfully displays the presence and power of an all-seeing and overruling God, who takes care of these little plants and causes them to put forth in due season.

As we were going up the mountain about three miles from home, where blueberries grew in abundance, we found roads in different places in the woods which were daily traveled by bears. William Howe, a brother of Lucy, being then with us, we concluded we would take a few of them, if they would please to let us. We went to work in the woods and made several log traps, such as are called by hunters dead-falls, as they were built in such a manner that when a bear came to one of them and wanted the bait, he would have to go in such a way that while he took hold of it, the trap would fall, and generally kill him immediately.

I had two steel traps, which I set also at one time. When I was gone from home, William went and found a steel trap gone; he returned home, and taking another man with him, pursued the remainder of the day, but overtook nothing. Early the next morning they again set out, and following, found where the animal with the trap had lain the preceding night; they chased him all day, but could not overtake him, and returning home-ward, came into one path some distance above, where we had set these traps, and when passing them, in the dark, they heard a great noise, which seemed to them that an old bear was cufling her cub, he cried and took on in so lamentable a manner. William was anxious to go and see what was the matter with them, but his companion would not suffer him, as he was better acquainted than William, and knew that if a cub was there confined and its mother was chastising him for his imprudence, she would be likely to show them some signs of her displeasure. They came home, and voluntarily said they would not go again after him.

Having that night returned home myself, and receiving directions from them in regard to the route, and not feeling satisfied to have such a loafer make off with my property,—he all the while suffering with pain, while in his thievish act,—I concluded to go and look for him. Accordingly, the next morning, in company with my brother Thomas, I set out, and soon found where he had lain the second night; we continued to pursue him as closely as we could trace him by the marks he made on the bushes, by breaking them with the trap, and laying the green brake leaves, which grow common here. I guess he began to think that Ethan, the Old Hunter, was after him in good earnest, and he was driven so hard and so closely, that he probably concluded to seek out for himself a good place, and then give us battle, as it appeared from the situation he was in when we overtook him. He was in a thicket, dangerous to encounter, for he was one of the long legged kind, savage in disposition, and now being covered, I thought it best to look out for him. Thomas, coming up with the gun, was desirous of demonstrating his skill in shooting him, but as the gun had been injured by hitting it against a tree, it could not be fired easily; he however aimed at the bear's head, but to his astonishment the ball entered his fore foot, the one he had at liberty. Beginning to fear for his safety, I took the gun and reloaded it, held the lock, the affected part, firmly in my hand, and firing, fortunately shot him through the head; he keeled over and soon died. We now released the trap from his foot, which was nearly worn off. He had managed to carry the trap and walk on three legs, on logs and over windfalls, by carrying it entirely up and clear of them. The trap when he first stepped into it was fastened with a chain and grapple; this he broke, leaving behind all but a few links, and that part which adhered to the trap did not trouble him much. We stripped him of his skin and then returned home with it and the trap, feeling justified for our humanity in releasing him from misery.

Early the same morning, William went to find out what had been the trouble the evening before, and when he came to the place, he found a small cub caught by one hind foot; it appeared true what they had heard the night before; the trap was in a measure torn to pieces, and the dirt and other stuff seemed to indicate that an old bear had been there sure enough, but did not happen to release the young one. As this cub was small, it was suffered to go entirely through, excepting one hind foot, and when he took hold of the bait, the trap fell and caught his hind foot. William took hold of him and bound up his ivory, then securing his feet to keep him from scratching, brought him home alive, thinking he might be tamed and made a pet, as he seemed not much hurt, and being so young and small he supposed he might be taught as much as any other of his kind. He would also make a curiosity, as he was actually a native of the place; but either the hurt, or the different position in which he traveled from what he had been accustomed to, affected him, or else he intended to show proper resentment, and he died, shortly after being brought home, notwithstanding he bathed him in cold water and gave him water to drink. His skin was taken off and fastened to the barn.

Shortly after this, word came about the middle of the day, that there was a bear in a trap. A party from the west having just arrived, one of the gentlemen said he would go and shoot him; accordingly, we, with others, mounted horses and galloped off. On arriving at the spot, we found a good sized bear in a steel trap. The gentleman chose his distance, and this was not far, of course, as he did not apprehend any danger from the enemy now before him, for Ethan was close behind. He fired three times, resting his gun and trembling as if he were freezing, (for any one under such untried circumstances would naturally have tremor of the nerves, although naturally brave and determined,) and after the third shot, I took a club or lever, and finished the matter of killing him; then placing him on my horse behind, brought him home, as this was the way I was accustomed to carry game home.

Once, when going out, I found a good sized, fat, short-legged bear in a steel trap, and having a small gun, with only a partridge charge in it, I stepped up to him and put the whole contents of the gun into his face; he fell back and died immediately. It was always against my principles to keep wild animals in misery, when they were in my power, or to try to sport with or torment them, (further than to try their strength), because they

were savage by nature ; but I would relieve them from
pain as soon as possible. I considered they had feelings,
and were not to blame for the species to which they belonged, therefore I had no right to do so; but I would
treat them as well as I could. This bear weighed three
hundred, and I had some difficulty in getting it on my
horse. Some horses are afraid of them and sometimes
get frightened by them ; this was the case with the one
I had, for whenever I made an attempt to put the bear
on her, she would snort and jump about in such a manner, I could not get him on. I then pulled off my coat,
blindfolded her eyes, put the bear upon a stump, tied the
horse close by, her head to a tree, and then putting my
shoulder under the bear, lifted him on the saddle. I afterward rolled him back on behind, loosed the horse and
then mounted the saddle myself, took off the blinders,
and went on home. Perhaps we made rather an awk-
ward appearance, but as my companion was now civil, I
had no reason to complain. Still it required some care
and management to keep the balance of him, and look
out for the horse, for she would turn her head round and
see her burden, snort and stop short, and appeared to
feel quite dissatisfied and uneasy with her load. This
we dressed nicely, but the flesh was not of much use to
my family, as there was an antipathy to it at home, in
consequence of stories respecting their barbarous conduct
sometimes, when they get hungry and tear to pieces human flesh and devour it. No one would eat of the bear
when cooked, although it smelled and tasted well. We
managed to save the oil of what flesh we could not give
away to our neighbors.

At another time, when going out to this now celebrated place for bears, I found a good sized yearling bear
caught in a steel trap by one of his fore feet, and he appeared not to have been long there. He had fastened
the grapple to a bunch of roots, and there was a chain
between the grapple and the trap ; here he was sitting in
an humble and ashamed-looking position. I looked him
over and at length concluded to contrive means to lead
him home. I cut a round stick ten feet in length, sufficiently large and stout to lead him with ; then taking
the throat-latch from the bridle, the stirrup leather and
the mail straps from the saddle, set the horse at liberty,
and managed to get hold of the bear's hind feet ; these I
straightened and tied to a tree. I then went up to his
head and secured his mouth, but not so tight but that he
could lap water. While thus engaged, in spite of all my
care, he put out his fore paw, the one that was at liberty,
and placed it so hard against one of my legs, that I really think had it not been for a good strong boot, he would
have torn the skin, but the boot prevented him from
tearing my leg ; he, however, took a piece of my panta-
loons with him ; still I would not give up the idea of
bringing him home alive. I then fastened a strap around
him, before and behind, and the stick upon his neck,
loosened his feet and began to try to lead him ; here we
had a great struggle to see which was the stronger, and
which should eventually be master ; and he played his
part so well I could do nothing with him ; he would turn
upon me and fight me all he possibly could. I now
thought I must kill him, but as I had never been beaten
by a wild animal, I was unwilling to give up now. He

would come to a tree and hold on, so that I found I could not lead him. I again contrived a way to confine him, but with more difficulty than before, as his feet were entirely free, and being quick and active with them, I had hard work to get them again, but after a while, I made out to. I tied his hind and fore feet together in such a manner that he could not scratch me, then placing him on my shoulder, with one hand hold of his ear, to keep his head from coming too near mine, in case he wished to make a little closer friendship, I trudged on; but he was so heavy and ugly to manage that it made me sweat, and I was obliged to lay him down often and rest, and whenever I came to water, I would let him lap it. I made out to get two miles, he all the while growing worse and worse. At last he actually turned upon me and entered into an engagement with me by scratching and trying to bite, and after tearing my vest, I concluded I would once more lay him down,—and the way was not easy,—lifting him up as high as I could, I let him fall, and the ground being hard, the breath left his body. Here I left him and went home, and sent a man after him.

This fall, at that place, we caught ten bears, for which I had three dollars premium apiece, and the skins were worth about as much more, which paid me pretty well for my time and trouble.

As we were passing back and forth through the woods, we discovered signs of sable. As they appeared plenty, I thought it expedient to catch them and make merchandise of them, their fur, at this time, bringing a high price, for the fur of those sable which live in this cold region is much better than the fur of those of a milder climate, and superior in quality. I hired two men and went with them myself into the woods. We set up traps, spotted trees to make a line that might be followed again, several miles in length, and then selecting from a flock of sheep the oldest and poorest, such as we thought would hardly winter for age, killed a number, and took them for bait. This business we stuck closely to while in the season for it, but it did not last long, as the snow falls early on the mountains, and a small depth of snow with a warm day and cold night, would freeze the traps, so they would suffer being robbed without any resistance.

At one time when William was going round to these traps, he found a live sable in one of them, which, from its appearance, had just got in. This was a pretty creature. He was three miles from home, and knowing their dexterity and fondness for mice, and being infested with rats at the house, he thought he would bring him home alive, and try an experiment with him. So he pulled off his mitten, put him in head foremost, then placing him snug in his coat pocket, went on his way. The little fellow being warm and comfortable, enjoyed it quite well. When he got home, we tied a cord around his neck two or three yards in length, and then let him go. He did not seem wild, but would partake of food such as was set for him. We put him in the cellar, and he soon cleared out the rats. He soon became satisfied with our treatment toward him, and, gnawing off the string which left the cord around his neck, climbed a window that was cracked a little, made a hole through it, and escaped. He appeared to understand longitude, as he steered di-

6*

rectly back, and the first time after this on going to the traps, we found him in the next one to that in which he was first caught. Poor fellow, he was now dead, the cord still around his neck, and thus we knew him. These animals are beautiful in form, color and motion, more active than a cat; and their fur is excellent for trimmings.

This fall we caught about seventy-five of these sable, for which I realized nearly one dollar apiece, and felt quite satisfied for our work. We made considerable havoc among the wild animals, and a handsome profit from them, beside clearing the woods of some pernicious ones, such as might have troubled us had they been suffered to live, as they were getting plenty. We felt quite easy with the thought that we were mostly free of them.

While engaged in this hunt, we discovered a beautiful little pond about two miles back of the Notch House, one of the sources of the Merrimac. The appearance of this pond and its situation pleased me much, as I thought it would afford abundance of amusement for our visitors, such as were fishermen. Beside this, the way in which we traveled was through romantic scenery. Leaving the main road half a mile below the Willey House, and traveling in the woods half a mile, we came to a ledge of great height, impossible to climb; this we took a different course to go round. For beauty and grandeur it is nowhere surpassed by any spot, to me known, about these mountains. This pond was well calculated for moose, as here grew the lily, such as they were fond of pulling up, eating their roots. Beside, we saw signs and tracks of them recently made, but we did not happen to come in sight of any of them while hunting this fall, although one was heard; but it was dark and he took care to make off with himself before it was light enough for him to be made a mark for the hunter.

This winter, 1830, I had business at Colebrook. I here found a man who had accidentally come across a hollow log, containing a nest full of young wolves; two of them he saved alive and tamed; these were so well domesticated that I thought it would gratify our friends and add to the novelty of our scenery to have such an animal with us. I engaged him for the next summer. He was so docile in the spring as to suffer himself to take a seat in the stage to Lancaster; then word was sent me to come for him. I went and led him home without any inconvenience, excepting when crossing the tracks of rabbits, he would jump and try to follow them and I would have to hold him fast by his chain. I brought him safely home, and fastened him in the blacksmith's shop in full view of any one who chanced to pass. Our little boy tutored him, and would make him howl whenever he desired. We found that when fed on animal food, he was more savage than when fed upon milk. I never but once had any trouble with him, and then when going into the shop door, I stepped upon a bone which he had just buried in the dirt, and he made a violent attack upon me; I chastised him severely, and ever after he remembered it, and whenever I came near, he would appear humble, obedient and fawning. He was as playful as any dog, but he did not like strangers quite as well; if they came near while he was eating, he would then appear cross, but he never hurt any one.

I bought a beautiful deer which I kept this summer, and a handsome peacock; these all amused our visitors. But there was in the wolf, a kind of shy, mischievous disposition lurking within, and whenever he could get a chance, he would lie still and seem to be friendly; if a chicken would pass his way, and if he came within his reach, he would make a sudden jump and take him; and the sheep, when they passed his door, he would try hard for one of them. At one time, I tied a long rope to the end of his chain, and let him into the hog yard where there was a number of swine, and an old one, who had young pigs, went at him in full rage, so much that she would not suffer him to take one of her young ones, nor give him any quarter. At another time we let him chase the calves in this way, with a rope tied at the end of his chain, and he would have succeeded in killing one of them, if he had been permitted. The deer possessed a mild, peaceable, inoffensive disposition, letting any one go near her, and would eat bread from the hands of any one, she was so tame and gentle; but let strangers go into her pen and take her by one of her hind legs, and they could not hold her; such was her strength and dexterity, that she would get away from them, do the best they could. The peacock was another favorite; he was a full grown one, and for beauty was not surpassed by any fowl whatever; he possessed a sort of pride in showing himself, and our little boy had taught him to strut, generally when he desired him. These animals were of no use to us and they were an expense, but I always liked to have such things to show to our friends and visitors, as they all seemed to be delighted in viewing them;

for they combined, as it were, the nature of the forest, and they, with the romantic scenery, always gratified every beholder.

This summer I had no great business on hand. I spent my time mostly with my visitors at the house, and ascending the mountains, whenever they decidedly requested it. But as I had been so many times up there, I was tired and worn out. I did not go when I could help it, but I always kept good and faithful guides, and every other accommodation that was in my power. The fame of this mountain scenery beginning to spread, and it becoming fashionable, many came to view these wonders of nature, and they were generally, if not always, satisfied, and considered themselves well paid for their time and trouble, and likewise they were satisfied with their fare while they staid with us. We used to tell them that whatever was lacking in substance we would try to make up in good will, and do the best we could to make them happy and their situation as pleasant as possible, and this never failed of having the desired effect of convincing them they were as much as possible at home. Among others, there came this summer four pedestrians from Boston, to spend several days with us, and ascend the mountain, fish, hunt, etc. One pleasant morning three of them proposed trying the hills; they were provided with a guide and everything necessary, and set off early, while the other one remained at home with me. As he had been up a few years before, he did not want to go again, and chose rather to try his luck in the forest.

A short time after they were gone, he took his gun and steered for the woods to a place where I directed him, and where I had in the spring put into an old rotten log some salt for deer; they found the salt and frequented it. Here he approached with great care, and soon had the good fortune to see a deer, and after shooting him, cut his throat, and with the assistance of another man, returned in triumph to the house with his prize. After performing the duties of a butcher, he hung him up to ripen, after which it was taken down and prepared for the table, at which he and his friends bountifully partook. During their stay with us I had a quarter of a fine fat bear sent me; it was caught in one of my traps, which I had previously lent a neighbor; this they also enjoyed very much. Here they staid and spent some time, enjoying themselves in various ways, and then returned home. This feat which he performed was told when he arrived home, but was hardly credited by some of his companions. He referred them to me, and I confirmed the statement.

I went up the mountain by an express desire from a botanist, to collect plants and save them alive, for I had been there so many times with a botanist to collect plants, that I had acquired considerable knowledge of plants, and the different places where they grew. I went over the hills and came down into the gulf, and then selected different species, such as grow nowhere else except in the cold climate of Greenland. I carefully took them up with a quantity of earth and brought them home, placed them in a vase with some moist moss to preserve them, and then labelled the vase and sent it immediately to Boston. It was safely conveyed, and the plants were placed in a botanical garden; how many of them survived I cannot tell, as I never heard from them afterward. The plants that were sent to New York the year before perished by the way, or rather some of the delicate ones. This was a beautiful employment, which I always engaged in with much pleasure; finding out how curiously Nature had formed them and put them in different places, according to their merits, or properties, and the state of the atmosphere in which they were destined to live.

This summer I guided several parties to the Pond. The first time I went there, we caught in a short time, about seventy nice salmon trout; they differed a little from our common river trout, as they had a redder appearance, and their taste and flavor was delicious. On the bank of the Pond we struck up a fire, and after dressing a sufficient number of them, we cooked them in real hunter style. I cut a stick with three prongs to it, and put the trout on these prongs in form of a gridiron, and I broiled them over the fire; then I would cut pieces of raw pork and broil them in the same way, and lay them on top of the trout, and that would give them the right relish. When cooked in this way, with a piece of good wheat bread, they made a good meal. I always enjoyed these and similar feasts in the woods, as in such ways I suppose our forefathers lived, when they first came over and settled this country. We had no fears from the natives, as I expect they had in that time, but we could eat and drink without fear of being troubled. All the fish which remained after we had eaten, I took up and brought home. My visitors, I believe, were as well satisfied as myself in all these excursions, wild as they were; at least they would express themselves so.

This fall we again set our sable traps and caught a number of sable, but not so many as we would have done, had it not been for the black cat, or fisher, who got the art of following the line and robbing the traps of bait, and would not then be satisfied, but would take the sable from the trap and eat them. This we did not like so well, but it so happened that we could not help ourselves ; they escaped being caught, although we tried hard to catch them, but they were so cunning or lucky we could not do it.

The wolves had been for a long time troubling us, and were actually so cunning I could not catch one of them, although I had, in various ways, tried. The nearest I came to catching them, was by setting a trap in the water in a particular place where they frequently crossed the river. One of them sprung the trap, but it was cold weather, and ice had gathered upon it; it did not shut so closely but that he pulled out his foot, and lucky for him, he made his escape. One good haul I made while setting the trap here in the water. It so happened that a family of ducks were swimming along, and they being so near together, four of them were caught at the same time in one trap. This, we thought, was almost a miraculous thing, but it is true, for I took them all out myself and carried them to the house.

In December there came a number of wolves to visit my flock in the night, but the sheep retreated, and went under the shed, and got in among the cattle and carriages. Their enemy did not venture in there, although they went as far as the middle post of the shed, for we tracked them there in the morning ; yet they satisfied their craving appetites, in a measure, by going just back of the stable and digging up the old carcasses of bears, which had been thrown there a few months before; these they gnawed close to the bone. The dog being shut up in the house, began to be uneasy and tried to get out, and, at length, I arose and let him out of doors, not knowing the cause of his uneasiness. He flew at them and they retired a few rods and then entered into an engagement with him, and I really think they would have made a finish of him, had I not interfered and driven them away. This was by a bright moonshine, and the dog, after being first liberated from them, ran toward me, and the wolves followed closely behind him, until they came near me. As I had no weapon to fight them with, being in my night dress, I observed to them that they had better make off with themselves, or I would prepare for them, and that pretty soon. They then turned about and marched away, but not without giving us some of their lonesome music. There were four of them. I counted their tracks as they made them along in a light snow; and it was just day-light. As my sheep had been on the place for a long time, and had taken a notion to ramble in the woods, they were troublesome to us, as we had to look them up every night, for fear of their being caught. I was determined to sell them and get rid of our trouble, which I did the second fall after this.

This winter (1831) there came some favorite hunters to go with me and search for moose, as we knew there were moose somewhere about the mountain, for two had been seen to cross the road a few months before, half a mile below my house. Everything being put in readiness, we with our dogs and snow-shoes set off. We first steered to the before mentioned pond. We traveled all day but we found no moose, and at night we went down to my father's; there we staid that night, and some of our party being wearied, remained the next day and amused themselves by cutting pasteboard mininoes, while father, Mr. Davis and myself went out in search of moose. We traveled another day, but with no better success than the former. We went up so high and so far into the woods, as to get beyond the living animals, such as we were then in pursuit of, as we could not see a track or a sign of one, and had actually got upon a hill, from which it was difficult to get down. We struck up-on a brook which had a smooth surface, being then frozen over, and father, sitting down upon the heels of his snow-shoes, commenced sliding down; he had got under good headway, when he came in contact with a tree which stood in his way, and, to save himself, caught hold of it; this, as he was coming with such force when he took hold of it, gave him a complete somerset, and turned him completely round the tree. We came down in a similar manner, but not without fears, as it was dangerous. We made out, however, to get in that night.

The next day, as our party which we left behind had got rested, we started for home, and on our way took some fine deer. These we felt justified in taking, as it is said that wolves follow when deer are plenty, and these ferocious animals had been troublesome, making great depredations among flocks of sheep in the neighborhood by killing a number at a time, and many more than they wanted for present use; but in my flock they had been more favorable, although at one time they killed and wounded seven; however, they generally took no more than they wanted at a time. They select the finest and fattest, and on him perform a curious act in butchering. We have found, after they have visited the flocks, a skin perfectly whole, turned flesh side out,. with no other mark upon it, excepting at the throat, where there was a regular slit cut, as though it had been cut with a knife, down as far as the forelegs; the flesh all eaten out, and the legs taken off, down as far as the lowest joint; the head and backbone left attached to it; the pelt left in the field but a few rods from the house. They would sometimes set up a howling, and a more terrific and dismal noise I never wish to hear than this, in a clear still night. Their sound would echo from one hill to another, and it would seem that the woods were filled and alive with them. ·

We had some trouble with the old barn that escaped the fire in 1816, as it had received some severe shocks in the times of the freshets, and had some considerable injury done to it this winter. We had fears lest the wind would blow it over, and destroy or injure the cattle; however, we propped it up, and it did not fall. I went to work and bought a sufficient quantity of lumber, and brought it home for a new barn. In the spring and summer I built a new one, sixty feet long and forty wide. This I set back of the shed, and I had a communication through from the shed into it, which made it convenient for all the buildings.

This summer we had a great many visitors, and among others, a member of Congress, Daniel Webster. It was in the warm weather of June, and he desired me to go with him up the mountain, which I accordingly consented to, and we went up without meeting anything worthy of note, more than was common for me to find. But to him things appeared interesting, and when we arrived there, he addressed himself in this way, saying, "Mount Washington, I have come a long distance, have toiled hard to arrive at your summit, and now you seem to give me a cold reception, for which I am extremely sorry, as I shall not have time enough to view this grand prospect which now lies before me, and nothing prevents but the uncomfortable atmosphere in which you reside!" After making this and some other observations, we began our descent, and there was actually a cold storm of snow here on the hill, while below, it was tolerably clear, and the snow froze upon us, and we suffered with the cold, until we came some way down, and reached a warmer climate. We returned safely home, when he related his tour to his female friends, whom he had left behind to spend the day at the house. Here they stopped again over night, and the next morning he took his departure. After paying his bill, he made me a handsome present of twenty dollars.

I had bought a little piece of artillery from the company of militia in Whitefield, and put it on a little mound which was called Giant's Grave, just back, or at the end of the barn. This I had there for the benefit of the echo, for when loaded and touched off, it would make a great noise, as it stood up in the air above the level of the surface, thirty or forty feet high, and when the air was still and clear, would echo from one hill to another, and then the sound would float along down the stream until it all died away on the ear. This was really grand and delightful, and all who heard it were well pleased, and some used to call it Crawford's home-made thunder, as it resembled the sound of thunder more than anything else. It was said that this echo was similar to that on Lake George when a gun was fired there. This cannon was made frequent use of, and for no other purpose but to amuse our friends and visitors. Once it was loaded and filled so full and jammed in so hard, that it burst in touching off, and that put an end to this kind of sport then. We constantly had company in the season for it, and many were in the habit of making us presents, and among them we were presented with another gun, much superior to the former, sent to us by Mr. Gale and Mr. Gibson from Boston to Portland, and brought from there by a man who had been to market with cheese. This gun would hold half a pint of powder at a time, and the first time when we loaded it, we fired it off in the road not far from the house, and it spoke so loud that it made the house jar, and cracked some glass in the windows. We then removed it to the before mentioned place where the other stood, and there it remained a few years, till we had some men there who were helping us get in our hay. One night it was desired to have it fired off and one of them loaded it with more than a proper charge, and then put in gravel and drove it in hard, as he thought he would give us an explosion such as we never heard before; then with his match he touched it off and it burst and flew all in pieces. I then sent to Portland and bought another to make up this loss, and that I left with some other interesting things at the White Hills. Some seasons we have burnt three kegs of powder in that gun.

Company coming from all quarters, we now suffered for the want of house room, and many times our visitors were so numerous, that for the want of beds and lodging rooms, Lucy would have to take the feather beds from the bedsteads, and make them up on the floor and then the straw beds would answer for the bedsteads. In this way we could accommodate two, and sometimes four, and frequently she would give up her own bed and lie down herself upon the floor, as she was always willing to suffer herself, if she could only make her friends comfortable. But this, beside being unpleasant all round, was wearing upon the constitution too much, after toiling hard all day, to be deprived of a bed at night to sleep upon. But such are the feelings which many are subject to, if they possess obliging dispositions, and more especially when they are used to misfortunes, as we had been, that nothing seems too much for our friends. As it seemed that it was not intended for us to have enough to buy such things in abundance, as most of our visitors were doubtless accustomed to at home, therefore it became needful to do every act of kindness in our power. I was again advised by my friends to build an addition, which I knew was necessary, but which my circumstances, I well knew, would not admit of. I had been in debt ever since I came here to live, but I had never suffered any inconvenience by it, and I had never been called upon in such a manner as to make me any cost, with two exceptions; and after considering and reconsidering, I found I could have fifteen hundred dollars from the Savings bank in Concord, by paying the interest annually for a number of years, if I gave them good sureties, and having concluded to build, I mortgaged my farm and obtained the sureties required.

The roads were again good, and I expected if they remained so there would be more company every year; and as the situation of my house was such that it had a commanding view of all the mountain scenery around, and this was actually, as I thought, the only proper place for all those who desired to visit this romantic spot, although another establishment had been erected three quarters of a mile below my house for the same purpose which for its size and construction, was well enough, yet there was but a limited prospect of the mountains there, for Mount Deception stands between that and Mount Washington, therefore all who desired to see it had to come to my house and view it from there. All who acted upon principles of honor and justice, preferred this place to any other, those who lived here having beaten the bush and suffered every hardship and privation, which such a lonely place is subject to when new. I had done everything to open and facilitate a way to the mountains, and make it as good and convenient as I possibly could, therefore, in consideration of all these circumstances, I expected public patronage ; and I always had a goodly share, particularly of distinguished men, and always will be likely to, I thought, at my house, if kept in good style, without having all the affluence of a city hotel, as that will not be expected, so far in the woods remote from market; but always having such

things as are suitable for such a place, served up in a
proper manner, neat and clean, so as never to fail to satisfy persons of judgment.

It is said to be a Yankee custom, that when a man is
thought to be doing well, there is always some one who
wishes to dip into the same business, as other men think
they can do better, especially, if they suppose they can
indulge themselves by living easily, and, by fair promises
never to be fulfilled, make others work without pay
for their labor; so with a ·man from Jefferson, in our
opinion, and we have a right to our opinion, and to publish it, with proper motives, for the public good. He
came in the fall of 1831 and bargained for a place three
quarters of a mile below mine. I had been acquainted
with him years previously, and thought him friendly, as
most other people are, and, also, that he was, as we were,
friendly to the inhabitants around, when, one day, happening to be down where this man was, for he had come
to look over the premises, (which he has since left, and
which, perhaps, "shall know him" now "no more for-
ever,") and make a bargain for the same, I said to him,
"William, what are you here for, and where are you
going?" This, by some, might possibly be thought im-
pertinent, but it was a friendly way we had of calling
one another by the given name. He answered he was
going to Bethlehem to see some men there. I soon left,
and this man went no further than to Mr. Rosebrook's,
six miles, to the man who owned the place, and bought
it of him, and, in January, was to take possession.

This clandestine management was a mystery to me,
for we were pleased to have a neighbor near, and no dis-

advantage had arisen by the settlement, nor never would have, had this man only taken the right course. We might have been a great help to each other, as had been the case with others who lived there before him; but, instead of this, he took a different way to manage. He, in the summer, made use of my mountain road, where I had spent considerable money, and which I had labored hard to make for visitors and my own benefit, and thought as much my property as any other part of my own farm, as it was made entirely at my own expense, through my own land. To prevent encroachment on his part, I was compelled to make a fence and to put up a quit against him; and finding he could not have this privilege by stealth, he sent a hired man to have Richard Eastman, Esq., come down to his house, for he was there at our house, wishing him to intercede for him, and see if I would not then compromise with him, and let him have the privilege of my road. The Esquire told him it was then too late for this; he should have come to me himself before he had attempted to intrude upon my rights, and then there would have been no trouble in procuring this or any other favor, and we could have lived like men, and have been an advantage to each other; but, instead of this, he tried to live on me and the effects of my hard labor. After this he made a path on the back of Mount Deception, and then came into my road, advertising he had made a new road, shortening the distance to the mountain. This I did not contradict in print, and thus the public was imposed upon and I was robbed of what was actually my own property in this insinuating way.

7

When I first came to live here, there was a mail once a week from Maine, up through the Notch to Lancaster, Vermont, and it continued so for some time after. As the inhabitants increased, there was another mail route established from Littleton to my house, intersecting the one running through the Notch, and it was necessary for the postmaster to open it, divide it, and send packages to the directed places. I was properly appointed to transact this business, and then it run twice each week but now three times, each way, once in each working day, throughout the week, all the year. My neighbor having a desire to take this situation of postmaster, got a petition draughted and had a false affidavit sworn to, for the sake of wresting the office from me; this petition he carried about himself, to the industrious inhabitants, who had not time to read it, as they said, and were not aware of what they were doing, when they signed it, supposing that they were to have an office in their own town, and not disturbing mine. He succeeded in obtaining names of eighteen citizens and three selectmen, as stated from Washington, and this was another misrepresentation, as this was a new place and the town had not been organized; therefore they had no selectmen or any other officers, excepting some men authorized to receive public money for schools, and that was all they had the power to do. This is a copy of the letter from headquarters.

POST OFFICE DEPARTMENT,
Office of Appts. and Inst.
AUGUST 24, 1832.

ETHAN A. CRAWFORD, ESQ.

Sir: It is represented to this Department, in an affidavit, that you have, at divers times, detained letters and papers which were directed to Phineas Rosebrook. The Postmaster General requires your answer to the charge. It is also represented by eighteen citizens and three Selectmen of Carroll, that the present location of your post-office is very inconvenient, and that the people who depend on it would be much better accommodated by its removal to the house of William Denison. The Postmaster General wishes to know if you have any objections to the proposed change of site.

I am, sir, respectfully,
Your obedient servant,
* S. R. HUBBARD.

This made me some trouble, as I was under the necessity of vindicating my own character, in the charge laid against me. I went to Mr. Rosebrook, myself, and he could not say as it had been stated, but only to gratify the man, who was an office seeker, had he spoken as he did, and most of those who signed the petition said they were willing to sign one against it, if I wished them, but that I could do without assistance from them by my answering the letter referred to. However, he did not obtain his object; the post-office was not moved.

After getting through with my summer and fall company, in the winter of 1832, as I had made up my mind to build, we had a great deal to do. As we had our glass and nails, our paints and oils, and other necessary things, to buy and bring home, we did not get ready to draw lumber until March. We then went at it with two teams, myself with one and my little boy with another, and this kept us in employment nearly two months, as it required a great quantity of lumber, such as boards, shingles, clapboards, etc., from this same before mentioned distance of thirteen miles. In the spring, I hired men and went into the woods and prepared timber for a house, and in May, we raised it. It was sixty feet long and forty feet wide, two stories, with the addition of a piazza on one side, sixty feet long, two stories, and this fronts Mount Washington, east; north end, Mount Deception; south end, the beautiful green hill where deer live in the summer, since named Liberty Mountain, and whence they have frequently come down into the interval and there played and gamboled about in full view, and many times have gratified our visitors by staying some time in this way, and then galloping off into the woods. Again I kept salt in an old log at the end of the meadow, which induced them to come down there. I desired my men never to frighten them, or injure them, choosing rather that they should come this way, than to kill them. In the fall, this hill, like the surrounding mountains, is richly ornamented with various colors, which, if imitated by a painter, would make, as it would at any time, a handsome picture. And there is a one story piazza, fifty feet long, to accommodate the traveler, as he could drive up by the side of it, and step into it right out of the carriage. I hired six joiners, who went industriously to work, and before the last of July, they had their work done, and the painting outside was finished, so that it was ready for company, excepting plastering, which we postponed for another year.

This new addition gave us a great deal of room, which required considerable furniture to make comfortable, without extravagance; and I was under the necessity of buying all this, and it only involved me more and more in debt; but still I hoped to see better times, although I

did not know when, for I was continually going from one
expense to another.   Still I had paid away my money as
fast as I had received it, and, I thought, to good advantage. There was, I may say, another great expense
which still hung upon my shoulders, from which I did
not know how to extricate myself.   I was obliged to
keep a number of horses, for no other purpose than to
accommodate my friends a few months in the summer,
for them to ride upon the mountain ; these I had to keep
most of the year, on hay and grain when used, and they
were of little use beside this, the rest of the year.   Then
I had the most of my help to hire, which took away my
coppers, as I always made it a practice to pay my hired
help, if I did not pay other debts, for I always considered
the laborer worthy of his hire, and all those who depend
upon their own daily labor for a living, ought not to be
cheated, neither ought their work to be trifled with,
while they who trade and get their living by speculation,
deserve also to be punctually paid their due, although
they do not always have so great immediate necessity ;
but were there generally greater punctuality, there would
be less failures.   I have often heard it said that

> " He who by the farm would thrive,
> Must either hold the plough or drive,"

and sometimes I thought I did both; but it seemed I did
not get ahead very fast, though I made the best I could
of it, laboring myself all the time.   I seldom lost a meal
of victuals or a day, in consequence of sickness, and I
had no other infirmities, excepting at times the rheumatism, which I think was caused by working in the
water when living in the state of New York, and a

tumor which I then thought was the piles and treated in a manner for the piles; but this was a painful thing to me. Many times I suffered greatly from the complaint, without saying anything about it, and I kept it to myself for a long time. This, I suppose, was caused by going through so many heats and colds in some of the many and severe hardships which I had encountered while trying to do all I could for the public, and I sometimes went beyond my strength, and had I not more than a common constitution, I could not have stood it so long as I did. This summer we again had many visitors, and among them came a gentleman from Georgia, for his health. He had fallen in company with a party which, after making their visit, took their leave of him and us and returned, while he staid some weeks. As his health was poor, he did not care much about the society of strangers, choosing rather to spend his time in the circle of our family, while he amused us, giving descriptions of his country, and the manners there, which interested us very much. Sometimes he would play some tunes upon a violin, which belonged to the house, and after leaving, before he arrived at home, he wrote to us, informing us his health was improved by our mountain air.

This winter, 1833, I bought a sufficient quantity of lime, and brought it from Portland and Littleton, to plaster my house, also paper to paper it; likewise in the spring, the mason came and plastered it, and then we papered it. We had some other troubles with our neighbor, by his encroaching on our property, beside what I have mentioned, which I will not relate. Some may say I did not like to have a man settle down near

me; this, if so considered, was not so. I might have
had the place where he lived, twice. The first man that
bought the land, as he thought, put up buildings, but it
happened that he did not buy the lot which he had built
upon; this circumstance I was aware of, and I might
have gone to the right owner and bought myself; but I
had no disposition for an act like this. He afterward
went and bought, which I was perfectly willing he should
do; and, after a while, finding that he should not be
able to finish his buildings and pay for the land, he came,
like a man, and offered it to me, first, and wished me to
buy it. This, also, I was advised to do, by my father,
and he offered to assist me if I bought it; but I told
him that I did not want it; furthermore, I was willing
to have another establishment, so that the public would
not be compelled to put up with a Crawford, because
there could be no other place; and, if I could not do so
well as to merit public patronage, I ought not to have it.
One other reason induced me to have the place settled;
the more inhabitants, and the better the accommodations
at the mountains, the more people would be likely to
resort here, as they would be sure of being made more
comfortable, and would not be crowded; and, moreover,
they could have a choice. Sometimes we were full, also,
and desired some to go to our neighbor's, and they
answered, if we had but a spare peg in the house, why
they could hang on that, one night, and refused thus to
be turned away; so we would do the best we could for
them, and make them comfortable, if possible.

This summer we had more company than usual, which
kept us busy all the time from June, until the last of

September, and not one night were we without guests. In July, the 31st, we had seventy-five to lodge, beside our own family. Early the next morning a goodly number of the gentlemen mounted horses and set off for the mountains, in good spirits, while the remainder, many of them, staid and spent the day at the house with us. They all anticipated, the ensuing evening, a social and merry time, as they intended to have an innocent dance after the music of a violin, which was to be used by a celebrated player, as they had done the evening before; but alas! how soon may the expectation of pleasure, in this world, be cut off! They all reached the summit in good season, and, partaking of the fare carried for them. by the guide, and making such remarks as they thought proper, they, at one o'clock, began to descend. One of the party being a sea-captain, said he would be the first down to see the ladies, and instantly set forward. The guide called out to him, and told him he was going wrong, but he, either not hearing him, or else thinking he might steer his way here on this mountain, as well as on the water, went on, and they soon lost sight of him. The rest of the party kept together until they reached the horses, but saw nothing of the Captain; here they found his horse and the rest of the horses, and knew from this circumstance, that he had got out of the way. They then came home as fast as possible, and related this to his brother, sisters and friends, who were waiting his return; they were alarmed and felt anxious for his safety.

I was called upon and consulted to know how we were to manage to find him. We then agreed that a

fire should be made on or near the stream which crosses
the path coming down the mountain, in case he should
strike upon this stream in his wanderings, and follow it
down till he came to this fire; then there should be
some one there to assist him home, while I should go on
the mountain and search for him. We accordingly set
out; his brother was to take care and manage the fire
and then leave some one to blow the horn and be on the
look out for the Captain. I ascended the mountain,
went up Jacob's Ladder, and out through the woods,
that night, and called out to him a number of times,
but no answer could I receive; thus I wandered about,
calling to him, until it grew so dark I could see no longer. I then made my way down to a temporary camp,
which we had to accommodate us when at work on the
road, and here I staid the remainder of the night.
Early the next morning, while it was yet dark, I arose
and pursued after him with renewed vigor. I went
again on the mountain, and again called out to him, in
different places, but all in vain; no answer could I get,
and I found one might as well look for a needle in a hay
mow, as to find a man here on the mountain, unless he
had accidentally slipped and put out a joint, or broken a
bone, so that he could not walk. I feared that this was
the case with him, and when worn out with fatigue and
hunger, began to call loudly, but I came home without
finding a single trace of him. This was sorrowful news
to his friends and relatives, but there was still a hope
that he might find himself safe on the other side of the
hills, which was actually the case. Here we will make

7*

use of his own language, as he wrote it in the album after his return.

AUGUST 1, 1833. The inclination I felt to reach a warm climate induced me to leave the party with whom I had ascended Mount Washington yesterday. After half an hour's rapid walk I found myself alone, and a little time convinced me that attempting to find them was fruitless. I then found my way to the bed of a stream, a branch of the Saco, and followed its winding for twelve miles, through briers and over rocks, from one till seven o'clock P.M., and when the approaching darkness warned me of the necessity of a bed, I discovered an object more pleasing than all the wonderful scenery that had served (though in a slight degree) to while away my six hours incessant labor. 'Twas a log bridge crossing the stream in which I was wading. Following the road with renewed vigor, I arrived in an hour at Mr. Hanson's, when a bowl of milk and a good bed left me nothing to regret but the probability of uneasiness in the minds of my friends here.

This morning I left Mr. Hanson's at five o'clock, walked seven miles to Mr. Wentworth's in Jackson, rode three miles bareback to Mr. Chisley's, who took me in his wagon seven or eight miles to Gould's, in Bartlett, whence I made the best of my way to this comfortable, temporary home, having been absent over thirty hours.

JNO. S. PAINE.

P.S. So the mountains brought forth a mouse. J. S. P.

"GO IT YOU CRIPPLES."

Kennebunkport party obliged to leave here this day in

anxious uncertainty for the fate of our cousin and friend, Lieut. J. S. Paine.

C. A. L. AND PARTY.

With hearts light and gay,
On a fine summer day,
We arrived at far fam'd Ethan's place;
When the sun shone so bright,
And all filled with delight,
We welcomed with joy each known face.

Then we wanted to go
To the mountains of snow,
And look on that scene so sublime;
But our friends said "nay,"
'Twas a dangerous way,
And the rocks we should ne'er try to climb.

So we waited to hear
What our friend Paine would bear,
From the weather, the road and the sight,
But we waited in vain,
For alas! he ne'er came,
And dreary and dull was the night.

May he come in his glory
To finish my story,
And tell of his victories won;
Then with sun beaming bright,
And hearts bounding light,
We'll farewell to MOUNT WASHINGTON.

This poetic effusion was written by the accomplished Mrs. C. A. Lord, of Kennebunkport, as saith the Album.

It is necessary for all who ascend the mountain, especially for the first time, to be governed by the guide, as the distance of more than a mile is over rocks without any surface to make any path or track, and unless the stranger takes particular notice of the way in which he goes up, he may, like the Captain, get mistaken and take a wrong course.   Several years ago, when it was the custom to go out and camp at the foot of the mountain, then, early in the morning, ascend the hill, a young Vermonter with some others came and went there and staid, and early in the morning set out to climb the hills. There came on a thick mist of rain after they had started, but he being persevering determined to go on, and for fear he should lose his way when he should come back, laid up piles of stones, as monuments or guides, at proper distances from each other, so that travelers should not get mistaken or lost, which remain in honor of him at this day and have been of use to many, who were like himself, determined to pursue after they had undertaken it.   He, however, returned to the camp after reaching the summit, sent the guide home for new supplies of provisions, and there they remained until they had a clear day.   Such was the spirit of a Vermonter.

I do not recollect anything more, particularly interesting, that took place this summer, worth mentioning, but suffice it to say, we had plenty of company until quite late in the fall, and some after the snow had got so deep that they could not reach the top of the hill.

1834.   Now as I was satisfied, for the present, with building, I had not much business on hand excepting that of buying and bringing home supplies for the season.   I spent my time principally with my family.   Home, with me, was always delightful, after spending the day in different exercises and getting weary.   To be able to sit down and have half a dozen little ones come and rest themselves upon me, all of them having good reason and proper shapes, which was a great satisfaction to me, was considered a blessing. In April, one week after the birth of our ninth child, Lucy took cold, and as she had been accustomed to administer physic to her family, when unwell, she now thought she would prescribe for herself. She then ordered a dose of hygean pills to be handed her, and took a large portion of them ; but as these had not the desired effect, she took another, which, as her physician told her afterward, was the means of saving her life at that time, but did not restore her to health. She remained sick and feeble, with a slow fever. I then sent eighteen miles for a physician who came and gave her such things as he thought proper, but did not remove the cause. We sent and he came again ; but no better did she get. Her case was now a desperate one. The child, for want of proper nourishment, such as is natural for children, grew very worried and fretful ; this served to add another trouble to Lucy, as she had always been healthy and could satisfy her infants by nursing them, but, at this time, it only seemed to injure and not satisfy it ; and as she had the feelings of a mother, she said she did not know how to bear with its cries. A friend, a gentleman from Portsmouth, calling at my house at this time, when going on business to Jefferson, saw the situation of Lucy, and she having a brother living there, whose wife had just lost an infant, they sent me word by the gentleman upon his return from Jefferson, that if I would bring the child to them, they would take care of it. This information I received late at night and when communicat-

ing it to Lucy, she seemed rejoiced to think the child
was provided for. I brought up several objections to
her against parting with it; told her that if they nursed
it, most likely their affections would be so great for it,
they would not be willing to give it up; all these things
she could do away with if she could but know it comfortably taken care of. Her mind being fixed, suitable
preparations were made for its removal. My courage began to fail, and I asked Lucy if we had not better wait
and bring her brother's wife over here? She said, no, as
it would be a long time before she would be able to come,
and she could not bear the sufferings of the babe any
longer. It was then wrapped up, and after it had received the parting kiss from its mother, which was imprinted
with a tear, for which she received a smile in return, for
the child was then six weeks old, I took it in my arms on
horseback and carried it sixteen miles, without a murmur
or a cry from the child, by stopping twice on the way
and feeding it out of a bottle, which I carried in my
pocket, which had been previously prepared for it. The
child was welcomed by its new mother, and after receiving plenty of nourishment, it became satisfied. I returned home and related my tour and good success in the
conveyance of the babe, and the satisfaction it appeared
to take in a new mother's bosom. This, Lucy said, was
an act of Providence, for which she hoped to be thankful. As Lucy got no better, I was advised to send thirty
miles for another physician, who succeeded no better
than the former one in removing the cause of her complaint. I likewise had the advice of several old and experienced ones, but all to no purpose; she remained

sick, weak and in great pain most of the time. She was told by her friends it was not likely she would ever recover, or arise from that bed of sickness; this did not seem to affect her in the least. She kept up good courage, as she was desirous of getting well, knowing that she had a large family of her own, beside Uncle William to take care of, and much there is depending on a mother in bringing up her children. These things she took into consideration, with a firm belief that God would, in his wise providence, see fit to send some means to help her; and after lying in this helpless situation from April until July, her desires were answered. Doctor Warren, with his family, from Boston, came to spend a few days with us; and his good lady, having been here before and learning that Lucy was sick, came immediately into the room, and seeing how she was, said she would go for the doctor. He came in and examined her, but did not prescribe anything for her at that time. He came the third time to see her, and then wrote a prescription for her, which as soon as it was obtained, helped her, and in a few weeks she was able to be about with her family. All this did the doctor, without receiving a single farthing, for he would not accept of compensation for his trouble or advice, for which we are still indebted to him.

Likewise we are under many obligations to a number of people of Boston, for their kindness, their attention and presents during the summer.

My affairs at that time began to look gloomy; sickness had ever been a stranger at our house, now it became an associate there. Our next youngest child was dangerously ill of the bowel complaint, and company began to shun my house, which was on account of the influence of stage drivers, as our neighbor, having made some addition to his establishment, offered to keep their horses on hay, free from any expense to them, if they would influence the company, and bring the passengers to his house. Of this I was verbally informed by them, but as I was then keeping them at a very low rate, I did not know how to keep them for nothing, and of course they removed their quarters. I had done much for them in making the place fashionable, which caused them to have passengers, who paid them handsomely for riding in their stages. This I thought would be enough to insure their patronage, without an explanation to them. The owner of the line had been promoted to some public stations, which should have insured better principles within his mind than to have let him practice upon such a low, narrow, contracted one, just for the sake of saving a trifle, and try to injure me in this way, at a time when I was in trouble. How much this added to their interest, or to the credit of the stage and its owner, I am not able to say; one thing I know, it was an injury to me, as I depended upon my customers for money to pay for extra expenses, which I had incurred by building, and making things good and comfortable for their convenience. Some people are so avaricious that they must have their own way even if it hurts the honest and industrious ones ever so much, as was the case, I think, with the one just mentioned. I, however, made the best I could of it, hired money to pay some debts, and other creditors I pacified with promising them they should have their pay as soon as possible. In the fall, as I was returning from Lancaster, on horseback, in the forenoon, I called at a six mile neighbor's, and there borrowed a fan, for the purpose of clearing up some grain, and when coming down what is called Cherry Mountain, the horse made a misstep, which brought him on his knees; being encumbered with the fan, I had not the means of saving myself, and I was brought suddenly across the pommel of the saddle; this struck an affected part of my body, and hurt me very much. The horse recovered himself, and I regained my seat upon the saddle. I went home that afternoon, and assisted in fanning up twenty bushels of wheat. Standing in the air, so that the air might carry away the dust which arose from it, and perspiring, I took cold, which settled where I was most liable, and that night my bowels began to swell and continued to for three days, and a man in greater distress than I was, I would think never need be. I neither ate more than three crackers nor slept the whole time. I had a high fever which caused me to be thirsty. I drank freely of cold water, which only increased my pain. I took physic, one portion after another, without any effect. I grew worse and worse, until at length, I told Lucy I must die; I had no desire to live in so much pain. She remonstrated with me, saying I had been the means of bringing a large family into the world, which was depending upon me for support, and I ought not to indulge such thoughts, but should keep good courage, and perhaps there would be a relief. I asked her when? Oh! she said she could not tell when, neither did I know how much I could bear until I had the trial put upon me. She told me to be patient and perhaps God, who had let me suffer, would in some way, cause relief. Well, I said I would try one more thing. I would take half a tea-cup full, or more, of Epsom Salts, dissolved in water; this was prepared and I swallowed it. Now, said I, if this does not answer the purpose, I must bid you and the children farewell. I began to pace the room; things looked strangely, and I had such feelings as I cannot describe, if I attempt it. This did not last long before I felt the salts begin to operate, and I soon found relief from them. As soon as I was able to ride, I went to Littleton to a physician and told him my case; he said I was a tough one and wondered I had lived through it, as mortification was near at hand at that time. He then gave me some medicine and advised me to be operated upon as soon as I could get a surgeon, or it might in time cost me my life. Other physicians, also, told me the same story. This I thought I could not live through; I still held the idea that I might as well die with it as to die while undergoing such an operation, for I thought it would certainly kill me.

In the winter of 1835, as I had expressed some desire of selling my place and settling my affairs with the world, in consequence of ill health, for I was not able to do much or go from home but little, one night in April, there came a man from Bartlett to make propositions to buy my place. He was then going to Boston, and knew of a certain stage company who would buy it, as he thought, and, in so doing, would confer a favor on me. I thanked him for his good intentions, then went to work and bonded it to him for six months, for ten thousand dollars; this he wished to have kept a secret, for a short time. My father coming in, before the close of the business, wanted to know what the man was there for; but as I had promised not to speak about it, I did not tell him. The old gentleman said afterward, if I had told him or if he had known it, he would have advised me better. In a short time the great cry of speculation in land· was heard on all sides, and I could have sold it for two thousand dollars more than I had bonded it for, but as I had never been in the habit of making children's bargains, there should be no grunting on my part.

Now to fill the place of the little one we had parted with the year before (as what I had predicted proved true, for those who had taken the child, unnamed, and nursed it so long, claimed it as their own, having no other, and we seemed rather compelled to give it up to them), we had another child born in May, which gave us ten in number, five sons and five daughters. Nine of them are still living. While in this solitary place, so far from human assistance, Lucy did not put her trust in an arm of flesh to save her, but she trusted to a higher power, and was carried through every trial, for which she had great reason to be thankful.

The man coming home from Boston, sent me word that I might depend upon the money before the time of the bond running out, and I made little other exertions to get money to pay my debts with, supposing this would be the case. As the bargain was so good, I thought there would be no failure upon his part, and depended upon it. He went again, and found a good company of speculators, who had money deposited in a bank in Boston, and every arrangement being made, the papers drawn, in the evening, for eleven thousand dollars, of which ten thousand was to be paid him, and he was to have a share with them of one thousand himself; the next morning, when they met again to close the bargain, no papers of the evening could be found. This disaffected the company, and they would do nothing more about it, as they supposed the man thought it was going so quickly, that he might have more; therefore, took no care of the papers. But the man says that they were lost by the clerk who kept the office where they did their business. Which of these two was the cause of this mistake, I am unable to say, but it was a sad one for me, as I had depended so much upon it, and might have done so much better, had it not been for my reliance upon this; but it seems to show the uncertainty of man and how little dependence can be placed even on those we think our friends. I always thought this man my friend, having been acquainted with him for years; but so it happened, and there was no help for it on my part. I was informed of all the particulars of this transaction by one of the company which thought of buying. I asked the man to give me the bond, which he said I might have, but I could not get it. He then told me he would try again to sell it, and still thought he could dispose of it advantageously both to himself and to me; but this was all a humbug. He still kept the bond, until it died in his hands. He, however, lost nothing more than his time and trouble, with the exception of what he intended to make, as he had not paid me anything for it.

During the summer we had a goodly share of company,

notwithstanding the stage drivers' influence, and that of some tavern-keepers, who were interested in this concerted plan of leading company to the wrong place; and many whom they did decoy came to my house, and said they were misled and should not be caught again in that way; but as I was then suffering with the complaint before mentioned, I felt little ambition about the proceeding of things, at times, but let them do pretty much as they did; and at other times I felt the abuse, and then tried to vindicate my own rights, but this I could not carry into effect, owing to the state of my mind, as this complaint centered in its effects mostly in my head.

After this, I strove to sell, but the fever of speculation had then begun to abate, and I could not get more offered for it than enough to pay what I was then owing, which was not as much as the buildings had cost; this I could not in conscience take, as the place was actually worth so much more. So we continued to stay longer and do the best we could.

My complaint increased, at times troubling me very much, and this winter, 1836, I was advised to send to Concord and obtain some of Dr. Morril's patent medicine, which was celebrated for effecting great cures; I was told that perhaps it might reach my case. I wrote to him, and in return, received the medicine, with directions. These I followed as nearly as possible, but it only made me worse, instead of better, having a tendency to heat and stimulate, which was contrary to the manner that my complaint should have been treated; yet I did not think any one was to blame in the matter. My friends being anxious that I should get well, said I must keep trying, and if one thing would not do, try another; this I did, but all to no purpose.

This winter, as deer had become plenty in the woods, many parties went in pursuit of them, and my eldest son, Harvey, possessing the same disposition as others, desired to go with them, but as his constitution was not equal to that of others, I did not consent to have him go with them.

In March, a gentleman came to my house, who had been traveling some years, and his horse being weary, he concluded to stay a few days and rest him. He being a sportsman, soon contracted for a little fun with Harvey; and as I had ever been against his going into the woods with others, I then concluded to let him go.

They were prepared, accordingly, and in the afternoon set out. They steered nearly south of my house, and went up the green hill where deer were plenty, and having arrived there in season, built them a camp, and spent the night finely, as they expressed it. Early in the morning before they had breakfasted, not being experienced hunters, as they were anxious to find what they were in pursuit of, they left their lodgings and victuals all together, and went out upon a tour of observation or discovery, intending to return and breakfast shortly. After leaving the camp, the dog went into a yard of deer, and followed them, and they found there was no time to be lost and were obliged to pursue as fast as possible, on snow-shoes, or they would lose both dog and deer. They soon came up with the dog, who had a deer; they cut his throat and took out his inwards' and left him there. The dog pursued others in a similar manner, and they caught three of them. By this time hunger began to call loudly upon them; as they had been in a hurry, and unmindful of the course they had taken, they were so bewildered among the hills that they were not sure what course to take to make for home. They, however, struck upon a small stream, and followed it down to the Amanoosuc river, nearly three miles below my house, leaving their game behind, tired and hungry enough.

The next morning I observed to them it was not customary for hunters to leave their game in the woods to spoil, and thought they had better go and bring theirs in, or else we should have to take their word for what they had done. The gentleman said he was satisfied to let his part remain where it then was, rather than go the route over again. He had had a pleasant time and a lucky one, in hunting, and found himself at home; he was then on good footing, and thought he would keep so. But as Harvey had for so long a time been wanting to hunt, I told him he must go and bring home his game; and after getting rested he took a hired man and went after it. He, not being yet satisfied, thought he would wander about, and perhaps might find a deer, one that he could catch and lead home alive, as I had done. The south wind beginning to blow strong, and the clouds coming on, it was dark before they were aware of it, and they could not find the camp, which had been built but two days before, where they intended to spend the night, and in consequence of the darkness they were lost, and could find no other shelter than a large hemlock tree. They had barely the means of obtaining fire, and

that was all. Their axe, provisions, and everything con-
ducive to their comfort, were at the camp, while they
were compelled to stay and draw out a long night, in
that season of the year. The wind blowing violently
made the trees writhe and bend on all sides of them.
The rain descended in great profusion upon them, and
they had nothing to shelter them from the impending
storm. But they were fortunate in getting fire in a dry
tree, which was some satisfaction, but not much comfort
to them, as all the good this did was to burn one side
while the other was shivering with the wet and cold.
The snow being deep, they had nothing to stand upon
beside their snowshoes, and in this perilous condition
they spent a long night. They said it was the longest
one they ever knew.

They suffered greatly from fear of being killed by falling trees, as they fell occasionally near them, but the
same Preserver who took care of them in sunshine,
cared for them then, and they were permitted to behold
the light of another morning with gladness, and in a few
minutes they found the camp, but a little way from
where they had spent such a miserable night. They
then provided themselves with a comfortable breakfast,
and, after resting awhile, started for home. They had the
preceding day gathered some of the venison, and tried
to bring it home, but the snow was so deep and soft that
their snowshoes would sink deep, and it was with difficulty they could raise them, and they were obliged to
leave it there, and make their best way home, where
they were welcomed. I think parents were never more
rejoiced than we were when we saw Harvey coming

across the field, as our anxiety had been so great through
the night that neither of us had slept. After that I was
not troubled any more with being teased by him for
want of hunting. He was now satisfied.

But to return again to myself. Sometimes I would
seem to be quite well, and then I did not mind my sickness so much as at other times; then there would a pain
catch me in the spine of my back, and run over me like
a flash of lightning, even to the top of my head, and
every hair would seem to move. Many times I have put
my hand to the top of my head, and felt the hair, to
know if it did not stand straight on end, as I could feel
it 'rise, and sometimes would think it would throw off
my hat. The pain from my back centered in my head,
which caused me to be forgetful. They who had ever
been my nearest and best friends had become my enemies, as it appeared to me, and from no other cause than
my being sick, and in trouble, when I most needed consolation, and this caused me sometimes to be irritable,
which was not exactly my natural disposition, but I
knew not how to help it then. My appetite was gone,
and I was attended by a cough, and afflicted by raising
great quantities of phlegm; my blood was reduced, and
I would have extremes of heat and cold pass through my
veins, one after another. Sometimes in the morning I
would think I could get up, and should be smart that
day, but after getting up, and only walking in another
room, I would begin to shiver with the cold, and have to
go to bed again, and have my pillows warmed and placed
on my back, and blankets warmed and put upon me. In
this way I lived' by turns, until I was returning from

8

Conway in the stage, having been down on business in company with Dr. Bemis, from Boston, and some other gentlemen beside him, when I was attacked with this complaint, and had, in the stage, two spasms, which required the strength of a man to hold me. This sudden and unexpected shock was below my father's, and I did not then think I should live to get home, but I meant to go along as I could. I had the kindest assistance from the gentlemen in the stage, and arrived at home, where I soon after had another spasm. Lucy sent immediately for a physician, who arrived, and took away a portion of blood, which soon relieved me. This kind and humane Dr. Bemis, who was then staying at my house, became acquainted with Dr. Rodgers, from New York, who had previously, before he started, been directed to put up with me, but was influenced by some other persons to stop with my neighbor. Dr. Bemis informed Dr. Rodgers of my situation, and he came to see me, told me unless I would consent to have an operation, I could not live long, as the consumption was near upon me ; said he would go and get his instruments, while another physician who was with him, should stop and make preparations for the same. This I did not consent to, neither did I refuse it. The doctor returned in a short time, and due preparations being made, went upstairs with them, when the operation was performed.

How estimable is the character of a good physician, or of any really good man ! While "man's inhumanity to man makes countless thousands mourn," so the kind ministrations of man to man proves that God gives us in charge of his angels.

I then came down with them, and soon found relief. I now could sit in a chair much better than for months before. The doctor came and dressed my wound several times himself, and then showed another person how to manage it, and when he took his leave, I asked him how much I should pay him? He said not anything, but he expressed a desire for me to get well. For this act of kindness I am indebted to Dr. Bemis for his interceding as he did in my behalf, and Dr. Rodgers for his assistance. I am well persuaded, had it not been for them, I should not now have been here a living man. Times had now become hard, and my creditors, who had waited on me, were afraid they should not get their pay, because my dissolution, as they thought, was near at hand, and in the course of the preceding summer they had come upon me like a set of armed men. I turned out all my personal property, even to the last cow, and some articles I turned out three times, I was afterward informed, but the state of my mind was such, owing to the pain in my head, I was not sensible of what I did. In the fall, before I was able to get about much, a deputy sheriff came from Lancaster for me to pay a sum of three hundred dollars, which I was owing the bank, and one more demand due a farmer for about forty dollars, principal, but as he had taken care not to have it reduced by interest and cost, which he had caused to be doubled, I told him I had then nothing to pay with, but desired him to be patient, as they were not suffering for the money, and they and every other creditor should have their honest dues, if they would only show me lenity. He then left me, after obtaining a promise, on my part, that as soon as I was able to ride, I would go to Lancaster and see them myself, and some days after, according to promise, I went, and what do you think these men did? Why, for want thereof, took my poor and emaciated body and cast it into prison, although a brother of mine and one of Lucy's, offered to give them bonds for my appearance at any time whenever they should call for me. But this did not seem to pacify them; they were determined upon other purposes; their object was money, and they refused to take them. I was put in jail, and this place was to me a complete hell upon earth, now shut up from air and the society of my beloved family.

My mind was weak, and the time hanging heavily, forced me to reflect on human nature; this overcame me, and I was obliged to call for the advice of physicians and a nurse. Here I was attended with a sort of spasm, similar to the former ones, and was really so unwell that one of my physicians affectionately told me he thought I should never pass the Gun hill that was near the burying-ground; that was as much as to say I should die. He then asked me if they should not send for Lucy. I told him no; it was enough for me to be there and not her. Here they kept me twenty-five days in this way. I had applied to an attorney before I went in, to make arrangements for me to take the benefit of the law, in such cases made and provided, and when the time arrived they told me I could not do it without perjuring myself. I told them something should be done, for I would stay there no longer. They then concluded to take our brothers for sureties, and let me go home. This added nothing to their interest, neither did it help them immediately to their pay. They were secured before. I had good signers with me on the notes, and my farm was holden, but when a man gets going down hill, it matters not what shape it is in, there are enough standing ready to give him a kick and help him down. They have since got their pay, but the tanner dares not look me in the face and say, How do you do? but passes by as soon as convenient; they will have to answer to their Judge. Lucy wrote to him in the most affectionate terms, intreating him in the name of a husband and a father to go and see me, and advise some means to let me come home, and sent it by the hand of her son, who handed it to him; he read the contents, and put the letter in his pocket, and never came near me till the day that I was set at liberty.

Having been for so long a time racked with pain, and having now these troubles, I did not seem to get much better of my complaint, and was advised by some friends and my family to give up my farm and retire to a more secluded spot, where health might be regained. Accordingly, for that present time, I changed situations with a brother of Lucy's, and moved to Guildhall, in Vermont, the place of our nativity.

Before we left we sent to those men to whom I had mortgaged my farm, to come and take possession of it, which they did, and I suppose, in a lawful manner, put up an advertisement in the house to sell it on the 16th of March, 1837. It was then subject to two mortgages, Uncle William's was one and the other was theirs. The amount of theirs was to be made known at the time of sale, but as it appeared, no one came to buy, therefore they had the whole management of the affair to themselves. At this time Lucy was there, and I expressed a regret to leave the place where we had performed so much hard labor, and had done everything to make the mountain scenery fashionable, and had just got in a way to make ourselves comfortable, and to be able to make our friends feel at home. It was hard to give it all up, and let it go into the hands of others. One of them made her this reply, saying, fifty years hence it will be as in old time; there would be those rise up who knew not Joseph, and it would not then be known who did all these things. They then rented it for one year, and at the expiration of that year rented it again to the same man for five hundred dollars per annum.

While we were at Guildhall, as there was a sugar lot on the farm, I thought I would make sugar that spring, with the help of my little boys, and as Lucy was always anxious about me when absent, particularly then on account of my health and misfortunes, I happening one night to stay away later than usual, she thought something might have befallen me, as I had only one boy with me, so after putting her children to rest at nine o'clock, she took a lantern and steered for the woods. Never having been there before, she lost her way and was actually under the necessity of calling for help. The boy having amused himself peeling birch bark, while I was engaged in boiling sap, we put some of this dry bark on the end of a pole which was long, set it on fire, and raised it up so high in the air that she saw it and then came to us and staid until we could all go home together, where we arrived at eleven o'clock.

We remained on this place ten months, where we raised barely enough to support our family. As Lucy's brother must lease our farm at the mountains, it being put into other hands, he was then wanting his own to live on, so I went down the Connecticut river one mile, and engaged a large two story dwelling-house, which was then unoccupied, for the farm had been rented to its nearest neighbor, and I obtained the use of it until April, when his lease would run out. Sometime this winter, a gentleman, by the name of Jonathan Tucker, Esq., who had an execution against the farm I was then living upon, came from Saco, Maine, and the marshal of the state came also, and set off, to this Mr. Tucker, nearly fifty acres of the best part of the land, with the barn. This is the very place where our grandmother lived when she had so much trouble with the Indians. I have tilled the same ground where their little log cabin used to stand, which was near the bank of the river. Afterward, they or others built upon higher ground. When this land was set off, I asked Mr. Tucker if I might have the privilege of improving it? He told me to stay and do the best I could, and if it were redeemed he should have nothing more to do with it, and the defendant in the case had six months for redemption ; if it were not redeemed, I could have a living from it. According to human nature, in these days, reader, how do you think this man let us live here after the redemption ran out? I wrote him an account of our management and asked him if I might pay the lawyer who had assisted in obtaining this land? He said I might.

Thus we lived upon this beautiful farm, while we had

the privilege of raising every kind of grain and vegetable, such as corn, rye, oats, peas, beans, potatoes; and we had a first rate garden, surrounded with currants, gooseberries and plums. As the river went round this meadow in a semicircle and made a bow in some places, there was capital fishing, where my boys could catch plenty of pickerel, some trout, dace, eels, etc. This made quite a market place, as these fish make grand living when cooked with good salt pork. Here we could send our children to school, six and seven months in a year. One winter we furnished the school with nine scholars, our own children, for which we received the credit of the committee, for, as the law was, every scholar drew a proportion of the public money, and the more scholars there were, the longer the school continued. We likewise had every privilege which is common in towns, such as meetings for divine worship and good society among our own relatives and friends.

As we had always been used to labor ourselves, we instructed our children, when quite young, to be diligent in whatever they could do; and this seemed to be a great help to them as they could earn their own living, and being accustomed to work at home, they were not ashamed to go abroad. When they were not at school, those of them that could be spared from the farm and dairy, for we had cows and made butter and cheese, could support themselves at home or abroad, respectably; while I could do mason work, as I had assisted in helping plaster my own buildings and learned how to make mortar, and could, then, spread it well, and I could earn my dollar per day when I worked at my trade. In this and similar ways, according to the customs of New England, we lived on this beautiful farm, by paying the taxes and keeping the buildings in repair, which we consider to be an act of benevolence from this Mr. Tucker, and for which we will return our gratitude. There are but few men in these days who would do so much even for a relative, without some direct compensation from him, if nothing more than a promise, for which he never made me a request. But the fifth year a lawyer who lived in Lancaster, by some means obtained a lease of the place and we were obliged to give him half we raised on this piece of land belonging to Mr. Tucker. There seemed to be quite a contrast now, after living in the way just described and now obliged to go halves with this lawyer, which did not exactly suit my family, working hard as usual, when they had the whole before.

In 1843, I hired the large three story building, which was then empty, in sight of where we had lived twenty years, at the mountains, and here we are at the present time in 1845.

It may be an inquiry, how these things have come to be written? Lucy had been advised to keep a memorandum of things as they occurred, for there seemed to be something very extraordinary in our affairs in life, which was an inducement for her labor, in which she has taken great pleasure, in order to be able to show the public our way of trying to get a living, by dealing honestly with men, and having a clear conscience as regards my management with mankind. Moreover, the men to whom I had given up my farm, said they were willing for us to have it again, by our refunding them whatever they had

8*

paid out, with the interest and cost, provided Lucy would publish this history, which, after being published, she could sell and it would be an assistance. As we were then retired from the cares of other people and had nothing but our own family to look after, she found time.

It is the request of some of my friends to have a genealogy of my father's family. Abel Crawford is now eighty years of age, when this year, 1845, shall have passed away, and he was the first man that ever rode a horse on the top of Mount Washington. He was then aged seventy-five, and is now a well, stout, athletic man, capable of doing work and business. My mother, who was Hannah Rosebrook, is in her seventy-fourth year, enjoying tolerably good health, after having raised a family of nine children. Erastus, their eldest son, was born in 1791, and grew up a large, stout, and tall man, six feet six inches high when standing barefoot. After he was twenty-one he went into the State of New York, where he lived and married, and his wife had two sons, and then he died there in 1825; these two sons of his are now nearly the same height their father was when he was living. Ethan Allen is my name, and I am fifty-three, with much better health than when I left the mountains. Stephen was born in 1796, and he died when he was fifteen years of age, with the consumption. Everett has a wife and four children, three sons and one daughter, and lives in Jefferson, New Hampshire. Dearborn lives in Oxford, New Hampshire, and has a wife who has borne him ten children, six daughters and four sons. Thomas J. lives at the Notch House, which I built in 1828, with his wife and four children, all of

them daughters.   Hannah II. is married to Nathaniel T.
P. Davis, and they live in Hart's Location, with my parents, who have lived there fifty years; she has two children, both daughters.   Abel J. has a wife and one child,
a son, and lives in Jefferson, N. H.   William H. Harri-
son still lives at home with Mr. Davis, enjoying life at
his ease, without any care or trouble of a family, living
in a " state of single blessedness."   Uncle William Rosebrook, who was spoken of in the first part of this history, is seventy-two years of age, and still lives with us,
enjoying good health.   He never was married.   Lucy,
my wife, has had ten children, five sons and five daughters.   Harvey Howe, not having a strong constitution,
learned the art of making wagons, and has gone into the
State of Ohio.   Our second son died when an infant.
Lucy Laurilla, Ellen Wile, Eluthera Porter, Ethan, Stephen, Persis Julia, Placentia Whidden and William,
make out our number.

And now my friends, who have a little time to spare,
or whose health is impaired, come to the mountains and
make us a visit.   You will find us here, and there shall
be no pains spared to make your time pass pleasantly
during your stay with us, either in waiting on you or
giving you all the information in our power, and, as of
old, what we lack in substance we will endeavor to make
up in good will.   We gratefully return our warmest
thanks for the public patronage which we formerly received while at the mountains, and we still hope by our
united exertions to continue to merit it.   When you get
to Conway, if coming in that direction, you will find excellent treatment in a Temperance House, kept by Colo-

nel Hill, the postmaster, where you will have entered the mountain scenery, and where, in fair weather, you will see the ranges of hills, or mountains, rising one above another along the way, and when passing, reflect on the mighty works of God, and think what the labor of man, in a few years, has accomplished.

The town of Conway, situated about twenty miles south of the White Mountains, began to be settled about the year 1776, by emigrants from Concord, Durham, Lee and the adjoining towns. The glowing accounts which the hunters gave of the extensive tracts of interval bordering on the Saco river, which runs through the same, the fertility of the soil, the exuberance of its forests, especially its sugar maples and white pines, together with its numerous wild animals and fowls, all conspired to facilitate its settlement. At the close of the Revolutionary war, in 1783, Conway had become more numerously settled than almost any other inland town of its age and size in New Hampshire. Its early inhabitants, however, were obliged to endure great hardships in conveying their furniture and provisions through a wilderness of sixty miles in extent upon pack-horses and hand-sleds.

They soon began the lumber business by floating logs and masts down the Saco to its mouth, where they received bread stuff and other necessaries of life in exchange, the moose and deer at the same time affording them a tolerable supply of wild meat, and their white and rock maple trees an abundance of excellent sugar. The rivers and ponds were also well stored with wild geese, ducks and fish of various kinds. In consequence of these conveniences, the richness of its soil and its healthy climate, Conway has now become a very pleasant town, dotted with several handsome villages, and containing about two thousand inhabitants.

Colonel David Page, Joshua Heath, Ebenezer Burbank, John and Josiah Doloff, were the first who moved with their families to Conway. They came by the way of Saco, in the State of Maine, thence up the river and across Lovewell's Pond, to the Seven Lots (so called) in Fryeburg, which town adjoins Conway, and had commenced settling in 1764, by Moses Ames, Esq., and six other families.

It was at the head of this pond, which lies about two miles east of Conway, that Capt. Lovewell and his company fought their sanguinary battle with Capt. Paugus and his Indians, on the 8th of May, 1725, and in which both commanders, and three fourths of their men, were slain, consisting at the commencement of thirty-four Englishmen and eighty savages. These Indians belonged to the Pequaket tribe, inhabiting the country from the Notch of the White Mountains to the Great Falls, on the Saco river, about sixty miles in extent, which has borne the general name of Pequaket ever since, from that circumstance. The town of Bartlett, lying between Conway and the Notch of the White Mountains, originally consisted of several locations, granted to William Stark, Vere Royce and others, in consideration of their services as officers in the French war in Canada. Enoch Emery, Humphrey Emery and Nathaniel Herriman, began their settlement in lower Bartlett, just before the commencement of the Revolutionary war, their land being given them by Capt. Stark, for settling. In 1777

Samuel Willey, Esq., Daniel Fox and Paul Jills, from Lee, purchased a tract of land in upper Bartlett, and commenced clearing the same. Their horses which they had turned into an adjoining meadow to graze, became dissatisfied with their new location, together with their manner of living and started for home. Instead of following the windings of the Saco in the path they went up, they struck off in a straight line. In crossing the first intervening mountain, it is supposed they became separated and consequently bewildered. Diligent search was made for them but all in vain.

The next spring a hunter's dog brought part of a horse's leg into the road in Conway. From a particular mark on the shoe attached to the foot, it was ascertained to have belonged to Mr. Willey's horse. On following the dog's track, about sixty rods from the road, the carcass was found. From the appearance of the large extent of bushes browsed, it was concluded that the horse lived till some time in March. None of the rest of the horses were ever heard of. Mr. Willey, not liking his situation in Bartlett, sold his land there soon after the loss of his horse, and purchased an original right in Conway, where he lived an independent farmer, until his death on the 14th of June, 1844, at the age of ninety-one years, being the last original male inhabitant of that town. An anecdote of him is considered worth relating here. Owing to the scarcity of provisions among the early settlers and the vigilance of the hunters, moose and deer soon became scarce; but bears remained numerous for a long time and are yet somewhat plenty. These animals often proved an intolerable nuisance to the farmers, destroying their sheep, hogs and other creatures.

One night in the summer of 1800, Mr. Willey was waked from his sleep by the noise of his sheep running furiously by his house. Springing from his bed to a window, he discovered by the light of the moon, an enormous bear in close pursuit of them. Calling his eldest son, instantly, then a stout boy about fourteen years old, they sallied forth with their gun, and nothing on but their night clothes, to pursue this fell destroyer. By this time the sheep had made a turn and were coming, pell mell, toward the house with the bear at their heels. Secreting themselves a moment until the sheep had passed, Mr. Willey sprang forth with his gun to salute his ursalean majesty. Old bruin, stopping to see what his ghostly visitor meant, was instantly fired at and severely wounded. Mr. Willey and his boy, with their axes, offered him a closer combat, and he readily accepted the challenge. After two or three charges they considered it the better part of valor to retreat to the house, which they did, closely pursued by the bear. While they were in the house reloading their gun, the enraged animal went round to a back window, through which he endeavored to enter the house, to be revenged of his antagonists. The room adjoining being dark, and Mrs. Willey supposing the bear to be on the other side of the house, in attempting to look out through the window, put her head within a few inches of his nose. On discovering her perilous situation, she gave one of those piercing female shrieks which make the welkin ring, and fell back on the floor. By this time they had reloaded their gun and now issued forth to renew the combat. But owing to the bad state of the powder, they were unable to fire the gun again. Perceiving the bear to be gaining strength, and now showing signs of an intention to retreat to the woods, after a few moments' consultation, they determined to make another desperate effort to kill him with their axes. Mr. Willey, after receiving strong assurances from his boy that he would stand by him, approached the bear a second time, and by one well directed blow on his head, felled him to the ground.

After passing Conway you will come into Bartlett, and I will give you some account of the early settlements there, as I received it from Richard Garland, Esq., in his eighty-second year. His intellect and memory are good now in his advanced age, and he says that in December, 1783, he was one inhabitant among five who came into that location, and that there were but few inhabitants for a distance of thirty-six miles, mostly woods, seventy-five miles from Dover, where they had to go for their provisions; and then they had them to draw on a hand-sleigh, in the winter, over a little bushed path, without a bridge. The people in Conway, when the streams were open, went down the Saco river in boats, or rather canoes, which they made out of a large tree by digging it out and making it large enough to carry several hundred weight, and when they came to a place where the falls prevented their passing, they would unlade their boats and carry their provisions and boats until they came to a smooth place again. At one time the inhabitants got out of provisions and sent for new supplies, and there came on a heavy rain, and the Saco river was risen to that height, they could not get back for some time, and those they left of their families had to stint themselves to live on seven potatoes per diem, until their return with provisions.

After some years this Mr. Garland had got a small piece of land cultivated, and it then needed plowing, and two of his neighbors offered him a team, if he could get a plow; he then went seven miles and borrowed the nearest one, in the morning, brought it home on his back, and his neighbor used it for him, while he, the same day, did a great day's work, at piling timber. At noon, he went one and a half miles and bought fifty pounds of hay to feed his team on, and this hay he carried home on his back; at night he carried this same plow home on his own back, which made him thirty-one miles, and half the distance with a load, beside doing a good day's work, and then, as he says, was welcomed to partake of the bounties which a kind wife had provided, and then could sit down in their humble cot with her and their family of young children, without fear or trouble. As they at that period began to raise enough to support their families, they had only seventeen miles to go to mill, and in the winter God provided them with a good bridge of ice, and in the summer they crossed the Saco river in canoes. His family in those days, as the old gentleman says, was a happy one; but he did not realize it then as he now does, while he can look back to that time when he would work hard all day, and at night come in and take his supper; then he would in the evening return to his work, and his wife, after putting her children to rest, would go out with him and pick up the small brush and keep him a good light to work by, until nine o'clock. She then would go in and make us a cup of tea, which we could partake of together, and then we could retire to rest, happy in our humble engagements, trying to get an honest living.

In 1790, in the month of June, Pequaket being incorporated into towns, Bartlett was incorporated, under Governor Bartlett, and called after his name. In August, they had a town meeting and chose town officers. Jonathan Tasker, first selectman ; John Pendexter, second ; Thomas Spring, third ; Richard Garland, first constable and collector of taxes in Bartlett. The next winter they had a school. Moses Bigelow was the first teacher of this school, of about fifteen scholars ; now they have their large schools, which will average, in the year 1844, over one hundred and fifty scholars, and they have one hunred and fifty voters in this small valley amidst these mountains. There was a time when one of these inhabitants had got entirely out of meat, and came to this Mr. Garland for some to carry into the woods, while he went and found some moose to make meat for his family. Mr. Garland gave him half he had himself, and then the man steered along for the woods, and in a few days, he returned as rich as any man could be, seemingly, with news of having killed eight moose, fine and fat. He then gave Mr. Garland three hundred pounds of this meat, provided he would take a hand-sleigh and go bring it in, which he did, and he now says that a bigger man never need be than he was then with this supply, great as it was, of meat.

As they had begun to make a road, some people in Portland offered to give any man a barrel of rum, if he would get it up through the Notch. Capt. Rosebrook volunteered his services, and went to Bartlett with his horse and car, and on the other side of the Saco made a raft, rolled on this proffered barrel, then stood in water up to his knees, and with a long pole pushed it across. He then, with the assistance of others, this Mr. Garland was one, put it upon his car and carried it up through the Notch, at least as much of it as was left through the politeness of those who helped manage the affair. This was the first article brought up through where the road goes now, and the first article of loading ever brought down, was a barrel of tobacco, raised in Lancaster by one Titus Brown, and the road was so crooked, they were forced to cross the stream, as Mr. Garland says, thirty-two times to get from Bartlett to the top of the Notch, where now is the Notch House and the post-office, where Thomas J. Crawford now lives. The first white child born in Conway, was Jeremiah Lovejoy, eighty-two years ago. Leaving Conway you will pass along through Bartlett till you come to Hart's Location. This was located to Thomas Chadbourne, by Governor Wentworth, under the crown of Great Britain, for services rendered by Chadbourne in the old Indian wars, and was called Chadbourne's Location. Chadbourne sold it to Richard Hart for fifteen hundred dollars, and then the name was changed to Hart's Location. Then you will come against Sawyer's Rock, which comes down near the river, so that there is just room for the road. This derived its name from the circumstance of Nash and Sawyer, when they first were bushing the path for a horse to travel in, through the Notch; they got down as far as here, and camped for the night, and in the morning they emptied their junk bottle of its contents, and Sawyer broke it against the rock, and gave it the name of Sawyer's Rock, and it has ever since borne that name. And this was the first temperance meeting on the Saco river, · or, so far as my remembrance is concerned, in history, in the White Mountains.

Some time after this there were two men riding on horseback, by the names of Blake and Moulton, and they saw near the rock two moose at play. They sprang from their horses and frightened them. They attempted to jump the rock, but the men, having the advantage, caught one of them by the hind leg, and with a jack-knife, cut off his heel cords, and hamstrung him. They then went up and cut his throat. As they were travelers and had not the means of saving the meat, they went down to Bartlett, and gave it to the inhabitants, who were glad to receive it. This happened, father thinks, forty years ago.

There are in this Location eight voters and twenty-six children under sixteen years of age, and they had a school-house built in 1844. It accommodates only four families, on account of the distance they live apart, and the rest have to board their children from home, if they give them a chance for a school.

Then you will come up to my father's. Here the stage stops and changes horses. Here the traveler may stop for a time, if he chooses, as Mr. Davis, last season, made a horse path from his house to the top of Mount Washington. This was done with considerable expense to him, and for no other reason than to accommodate those who might prefer going from there on the mountains, as they had several fine views in going that way. He charges the same as others do for guiding travelers up the mountains. Gentlemen and ladies also can ascend. Then you will, after leaving father's, come to what is called the old Notch House, which place was settled, Uncle William says, about fifty-three years ago, by one Mr. Davis, who first began there; since which period, others have lived there for a short time, until Samuel Willey bought the place, and repaired it. He with his family lived there, till that dreadful night in August, when all were destroyed by the great storm, described in the foregoing pages; then John Pendexter built the barn, and that stands there still, and he improved it. Other have lived there, by turns, until last season Mr. Fabyan made thorough repairs, both on the house and stable, and this season he has built a new frame for a house, seventy feet by forty, for himself, so that by next season, he may be prepared for company that, visiting the mountains, wish to spend a portion of their time at the Willey House. This place which is now nothing but sand and gravel, was over a beautiful valley, covered with maple, and there used to be a great quantity of sugar made there. Then you will come up through the Notch to Thomas Crawford's, called the Notch House. He has a road to the mountain, nearly in the same place I first traveled, which was the first path ever made to the top of Mount Washington. You will pass along to where a man and his wife were once traveling, with one horse, in what used to be called a pung, and met in their way a moose. The snow was deep, and he, thinking he had a right to his path, refused to turn out; but when they came near, the moose jumped over the whole concern and just cleared the woman's head.

Then from the Notch four miles will bring you to the old Rosebrook stand, where once stood, in or near the road, a shed seventy feet long. As some hunters were pursuing a moose, he came into the road and went directly through this shed, passed on by the house, and made for the river, and went down the falls, dislocating one of his knee joints. The hunters followed about three miles, caught him and made a grand feast of him. It was in those days no uncommon thing to find these animals at any time when they were hunted for.

This ancient Rosebrook place is thirty-six miles from Conway, eighteen from Lancaster, eighteen from Franconia, and a good road we now have over Cherry Mountain, where once was a good turnpike, and it may be traveled with safety both summer and winter toward Jefferson. This place, also, is eighteen miles from Littleton, and stages run six times a week alternately, coming from Conway Mondays, Thursdays, and Saturdays, resting on Sundays, and arrive at either place, at night, fifty-four miles apart. When you get to the old Rosebrook place, you are in the most romantic scenery, perhaps, this side of the mountains.

The reader may suppose me partial to this place, and well he may, as I have lived here so long, and have seen good times with my friends, who extend all over the land in every direction; from this place, also, we have a good horse path to Trinity Height, the summit of Mount Washington. Nearly seven miles of this road is over a comparatively level surface, and two and one quarter miles is on rising ground; and many have seated themselves on a horse at the house, and never dismounted until they have been to the top of the mountain and returned. This can be accomplished in six to nine hours. Parties often stop by the way and fish for trout. These in old times were plenty, and of large size; but in this day, having so many fishing for them, they do not have time to grow very large before they are called for. But they are excellent, although small. Trout is the only kind of fish caught in these cold streams about the hills, and not much game is left excepting deer, which live here yet, and are caught now and then by having good dogs to find and follow them until tired out; sometimes the dog kills them, sometimes the hunter. Sometimes they are driven to the meadow, sometimes to the pond, where they are hunted after in canoes, and taken or killed.

As in the providence of God, everything changes in this world, the weather now is not so cold as it formerly was. We have now scarcely a week of steady cold, when, in former times, I have heard grandmother say, she has seen six weeks at a time that neither the heat from her log cabin, nor the sun would soften the snow so much as to cause one drop of water to fall from the eaves of the house. We now seldom have over two feet of snow at a time, and in years past it was no uncommon thing to have from six to nine feet. I have seen nine feet measured upon a level surface, and have known the snow to fall in less than twenty-four hours, twenty-seven inches. Yet we have early and late frosts in the spring, and early frosts in the fall, which prevent our raising such things as the frost injures; but we generally can raise good oats and potatoes, and sometimes wheat, rye, and peas. In 1820, I raised some sound corn, but have never since had any get ripe. There is not a better place in New England for cattle and sheep than this. Goats and mules would do well, but they are too troublesome.

We can now go to Portland and back with a team, in from six to eight days; in old times, it has taken twenty-two days to go from Lancaster to Portland, and back. The snow was so deep at one time that they were obliged to leave their horses seven days in one place before they could be moved. The average time of snow in the fall is about the first of November, and it goes off, generally, the first of April, so that about the middle of May, we here begin to plow and prepare our ground for raising such things as the climate will permit. Fowls do well here, such as ducks, geese, chickens; and the turkey here is excellent. We have kept pigeons, but they never seemed to increase to do much, only serving to amuse the children. Bees do well here and are common in the woods. They make the best flavored honey, as they have such a variety of wild flowers to extract their sweets from. As for pork, we do not raise enough here to support our own families, but depend on buying, principally, for our own use. There is some maple sugar made in different places about these mountains, but little in comparison to what there was in former times. And the probable amount of trout caught from one year to another, according to my judgment, in the Amanoosuc and

Saco rivers, is from six to seven hundred weight. The average weight is from four ounces to eight. There have been some caught here, forty years ago, that would weigh four and five pounds, and many and large ones now are found in the vicinity, in several directions. And salmon have been taken here, fifty years since, of ten pounds weight. Three or four hundred different Alpine White Mountain plants are found about here, and there are still found on some of the slides, near the Willey, or old Notch House, handsome minerals or crystallized quartz. There used to be great quantities of fur taken around these mountains, but wild animals have all been hunted so much, they are getting to be scarce ; but there is some sable or martin, and some few other animals caught every year.

I will give the minutes of the weather : —

1844.	*Sunrise.*	*2 p.m.*	*Sunset.*	1845.	*Sunrise.*	*2 p.m.*	*Sunset.*
July 22.......	38	87	60	January 30.......	*8	10	*4
" 23.......	67	78	66	" 31.......	15	*1	*5
" 24.......	49	79	60	February 1.......	*22	*2	*21
" 25.......	52	66	51	" 2.......	*33	*6	*12
" 26.......	38	70	56	" 3.......	*34	*8	*6
" 27.......	28	68	56	" 4.......	*2	10	4
" 28.......	30	78	54	" 5.......	20	18	14
" 29.......	54	78	63	" 6.......	6	2	2
" 30.......	50	71	64	" 7.......	2	4	1
" 31.......	64	66	58	" 8.......	*1	6	3

This is the register of the thermometer for A.D. 1844-5, when, on the whole, we had a moderate winter, for this part of the country, and the summers, in general,

*Below zero.

are not so warm as they were formerly. As the land is cleared, perhaps the winds in summer have greater range, render the atmosphere more pleasant; and in winter, snow that used to fall upon the stumps and bushes, and all level places, is blown off by the winds, and there is generally a cooler, more dry, and salubrious air.

THE WHITE MOUNTAINS.

WHERE TO GO AND WHAT TO SEE.

The White Mountains long noted for beauty and grandeur, have become the most popular summer resort in New England; and are yearly visited by many thousand people from every part of the country.

MOUNT WASHINGTON.

The highest summit of the White Mountains, Mount Washington, is 6,293 feet above the sea level, and in extent and beauty the view from it is not surpassed by anything east of the Rocky Mountains, including, as it does, a wide stretch of territory in New Hampshire, Maine and Vermont, with the ocean, and mountains in Massachusetts, New York and Canada, visible in clear weather. The Summit House, on the very top of the Mountain, accommodates two hundred guests.

The ascent is made by the railway from the west side, and the carriage road from the east. The railroad is three miles long, and has an average rise of one foot in four, the steepest being thirteen and a half inches to the yard. The grade is overcome by means of cog-wheels working in a cog-rail in the center of the track, and powerful brakes on engines and cars insure safety. No passenger has been injured since the road was opened. The running time is one and one-half hours, and only one car is run with each engine.

The carriage road to the summit is eight miles long, and has an average grade of twelve feet in one hundred. The ascent is made by stages in four hours, and the descent in an hour and a half.

THE CRAWFORD NOTCH.

The Crawford, or White Mountain Notch, is a narrow pass about twelve miles long, presenting some of the finest scenery on the continent. The Saco River flows through the valley, and for miles the mountains rise on either side over 2,000 feet. The Portland and Ogdensburg railroad, which runs along the mountain side, commanding a view of the valley, in the eight miles from Bemis station to the Crawford House has an average grade of 116 feet to the mile. Observation cars are run through the Notch.

The entrance to the Notch, at the northern end, near the Crawford House, was originally only twenty-six feet wide, leaving just room for the river, but was widened to allow the passage of a carriage road and afterward of the railroad track. A large rock just outside the "gateway" is called, from its shape, Elephant's Head. A little down the Notch on the east side are two beautiful falls, Flume and Silver Cascades.

MOUNT WILLARD,

Which stands just at the head of the Notch, is famous for the beautiful view it affords of this wild and picturesque mountain gorge, a landscape not surpassed by any in the mountains. The late afternoon is the best time to see the view. A good road two miles long extends to the summit. Hitchcock's Flume, a singular rock formation, is near the top of the mountain. On the precipitous face of the mountain, nearly a thousand feet above the Notch, is seen the entrance to a cavern known as the Devil's Den.

THE WILLEY HOUSE,

The scene of the terrible disaster of over fifty years ago, is in the Notch, three miles below the Crawford House. The house was occupied in 1826 by James' Willey jr. and his family. A fearful storm raged in the Notch on the night of August 28, 1826, and the entire family, fleeing from the house to a place of supposed safety, were buried in an avalanche of earth and rocks, precipitated from the side of Mount Willey. A huge rock 30 feet high, directly behind the house, parted the slide and saved the building.

THE GLEN.

The Glen House, in Pinkham Notch, at the eastern base of Mount Washington, is fifteen miles north of Glen station, near North Conway, eight miles south of Gorham on the Grand Trunk railway, and has a full and unobstructed view of the highest peaks of the Mount Washington range. Mount Washington is ascended from the Glen by the carriage road, eight miles long. Glen Ellis Fall and Crystal Cascade, near the Glen, are two of the finest waterfalls in the mountain. Tuckerman's Ravine is most easily reached from the Glen House.

FABYAN HOUSE.

The Fabyan House station is the great railroad center of the White Mountains. It is situated in the Amanoosuc valley, 6 miles from the base of Mount Washington, 9 miles from the summit. All express trains to and from the White Mountains arrive and depart from the Fabyan House. The distances east are : Mount Pleasant House one half mile, Crawford House at entrance to White Mountain Notch 4 miles, Upper Bartlett 19, Glen station 25, North Conway 31, Portland 91. On the west, White Mountain House 1 mile, Twin Mountain House 5 miles, Bethlehem Junction 10, Bethlehem village 13, Profile House 20, Flume 26, Littleton 20.

JACKSON.

On the east side of Mount Washington, and within three miles of Glen Station is the village of Jackson. It is a favorite resort of artists. Goodrich and Jackson Falls are near the village, and are both fine waterfalls.

NORTH CONWAY.

In the Saco valley, 31 miles from Fabyan's, and 60 from Portland is the pleasant village, with beautiful surroundings, of North Conway. It has accommodations for 1,500 visitors. The valley is inclosed between Kearsarge and Moat mountains, and a most attractive landscape is formed by the intervals and the mountain peaks, with Washington in the background. For beauty of scenery there is none finer in the White Mountains. The largest hotel is the Kearsarge House, and among the others are the Sunset Pavilion, Randall,

North Conway, Eastman, McMillan, Artists Falls and Moat Mountain Houses. Two miles north of North Conway is Intervale Station. There are several hotels, the largest being the Intervale House, near which are the Bellevue, Pendexter Mansion, and others. Bartlett and Lower Bartlett are a few miles above North Conway, on the Saco river.

HISTORICAL EVENTS.

Little is known regarding the White Mountains before the year 1642, when Darby Field of Portsmouth made the first ascent of Mount Washington. Indian tribes then lived near the mountains, but few of their traditions have been preserved. Their name for the mountains was Waumbek Methna and for Mount Washington, Agiochook. John Josselyn, in his book "New England Rarities Discovered," published in 1672, gave the first description of the mountains.

The White Mountain Notch was discovered by two hunters, Nash and Sawyer, in 1771.

The first settlements among the mountains were made in the latter half of the last century, Conway being settled in 1764, Franconia in 1774, Bartlett in 1777, Jackson in 1778 and Bethlehem in 1790.

Capt. Eleazer Rosebrook made the first settlement at the site of the Fabyan House in 1792. He opened there in 1803 the first house for summer visitors ever kept in the mountains. His son-in-law, Abel Crawford, long known as the "Patriarch of the Mountains," settled at what is now Bemis station in 1793. The latter's son,

Ethan Allen Crawford, the most famous of the mountain pioneers, took Rosebrook's house in 1817. In 1819 he opened the first foot-path up Mt. Washington. His brother, Thomas J. Crawford, opened the first bridle-path to the summit in 1840, and his father, then seventy-five years old, rode the first horse that climbed the mountain.

The first hotel on Mount Washington was the old Summit House, built in 1852, the Tip-top House was built in 1853, and the present Summit House in 1872.

The first winter ascent of Mount Washington was made by the sheriff of Coos county and B. F. Osgood of Gorham, December 7th, 1858. John H. Spaulding, Franklin White and C. C. Brooks of Lancaster made the ascent February 19, 1862, and were the first to spend the night on the mountain in winter.

The carriage road from the Glen House to the summit of Mount Washington was begun in 1855, under the management of D. O. Macomber, C. H. V. Cavis being surveyor. The first four miles were finished the next year. Financial troubles stopped the work for a time, but the road was finally opened August 8, 1861.

George W. Lane, now in charge of the Fabyan House stables, drove the first Concord coach that ever ascended Mount Washington, August 8, 1861, on the opening of the carriage road. It contained J. M. Thompson, then proprietor of the Glen House, and his family, including George F. Thompson, the present manager of the Wentworth at New Castle.

The Mount Washington railway was projected by Sylvester Marsh. The building of the road was begun in 1866 and finished in 1869.

The signal station at the Summit was established in 1870. Prof. J. H. Huntington of the state geological survey was at the head of the party that spent the first winter, having with him Sergeant Theodore Smith of the signal service and S. A. Nelson of Georgetown, Mass. The building now occupied by the observers was erected in 1873.

The first number of "Among the Clouds," which was the first newspaper published in the White Mountains, and the only one printed on any mountain in the world, was issued July 18, 1877, by Henry M. Burt of Springfield, Massachusetts.

MOUNTAIN TRAGEDIES.

The destruction of the Willey family by a land slide in the White Mountain Notch, occurred August 28, 1826.

Frederick Strickland, an Englishman, perished in the Amanoosuc Ravine in October, 1851.

Miss Lizzie Bourne of Kennebunk, Maine, perished on the Glen bridle-path, near the summit, on the night of September 14, 1855.

Dr. B. L. Ball of Boston was lost on Mount Washington in October, 1855, in a snow storm, but was rescued after two days' and nights' exposure, without food or sleep.

Benjamin Chandler of Delaware perished near Chandler's Peak, half a mile from the top of Mount Washington, August 7, 1856, in a storm, and his remains were not discovered for nearly a year.

Harry W. Hunter of Pittsburg, Pennsylvania, per-

9*

ished on the Crawford bridle-path September 3, 1874, a mile from the summit. His remains were found nearly six years later, July 14, 1880.

DISTANT POINTS VISIBLE FROM MOUNT WASHINGTON.

Below is given a list of the prominent distant points seen from Mount Washington, prepared from W. H. Pickering's articles on the subject, in Appalachia. The distance of each point is given, also its direction. If the points are identified by a compass, allowance must be made for the variation of the needle, which amounts to 13 degrees west. Thus, if a mountain's position is east of north or west of south, add 13 degrees to the given direction; if west of north or east of south, subtract 13 degrees.

Mount Megantic, 86 miles, north 1 deg. west, one-third the way from Jefferson to Adams; height, 3000 feet. Situated in Canada, in a comparatively level region.

Mount Carmel, sixty-five miles, north 12 deg. east, just over Adams. Near the northern boundary of Maine, and recognized by the steep slope on the eastern side.

Saddle-back, 60 miles, north 40 deg. east. Height 3,-700 feet. A saddle-shaped mountain, at the head of Rangeley Lakes.

Mount Bigelow, 82 miles, north 43 deg. east. It appears as three rounded hills.

Mount Abraham, 68 miles, north 47 deg. east. Height, 3400 feet. A long, serrated ridge. Katahdin, long sup-

posed to be visible, is hidden behind this mountain, and
2000 feet would have to be added to its height to bring
it into view. Should a distant mountain be seen in
that direction, it would probably be one of the lower
ones about the southern end of Moosehead Lake.

Ebene Mountain, 135 miles, north 50 deg. east. Seen
rising over a valley in the Russell Mountains, 103 miles
distant, which are themselves seen through a depression
in the nearer horizon. This is the most distant point
yet identified from Mount Washington, and is brought
into view solely by atmospheric refraction.

Mount Blue, 57 miles, north 56 deg. east. Height,
2700 feet. A conspicuous pyramid peak, near Farming-
ton, Maine.

Sebago Lake, 43 miles, south 51 deg. east, and over
the northern summit of Doublehead. It is fourteen
miles long by eleven broad.

The city of Portland, 67 miles, south 51 deg. east,
and situated just over the right-hand end of the broad-
est portion of Lake Sebago. The ocean cannot be seen
as often as are some more distant objects in other directions, partly on account of the difficulty of distinguishing
distant water, and partly because the atmosphere in this
direction is generally somewhat thicker than elsewhere.

Mount Agamenticus, 79 miles, south 23 deg. east,
rather more than two-thirds of the way from Kearsarge
(north), to Moat, and just over White Horse Ledge.
It has the appearance of a flat-rounded hill, slightly pro-
jecting above the horizon.

The Isles of Shoals, 96 miles, south 21 deg. east, appear on the horizon just to the right of Agamenticus.
They are rarely seen from Mount Washington.

The Uncanoonucs, 90 miles, south 10 deg. east, just over the left shoulder of Passaconaway.

 Joe English Hill, 93 miles, south 10 deg. west, lying half way between Passaconaway and Whiteface.

Mount Monadnock, 104 miles, south 23 deg. west, and one-fourth of the way from Black Mountain to Carrigain Mountain, and appears as a very regular rounded summit.

Mount Kearsarge (south), 27 miles, south 24 deg west, and nearly half way between Black and Carrigain Mountains, somewhat resembles Monadnock in shape.

Nelson Pinnacle, 97 miles distant is seen over the right shoulder of Kearsarge.

Mount Ascutney, 81 miles, south 45 deg. west, is visible nearly over Mount Carr.

The Killington Peaks, 88 miles, south 59 deg. west, are twin peaks near Rutland, Vermont, and are seen on the horizon between Moosilauke and Lincoln. The southern one is called Killington, and the northern, Pico.

Camel's Hump, 78 miles, north 87 deg. west, appears slightly to the left of Fabyan's. It is one of the highest of the Green Mountains, and is shaped like a truncated cone, with very steep sides. It is plainly visible at sunset on a clear day.

Mount Whiteface, 130 miles, north 86 deg. west, rises over the right hand slope of Camel's Hump. It is 4900 feet high, one of the highest of the Adirondacks.

Mount Mansfield, 77 miles, north 76 deg. west, between the Twin Mountain House and Mount Deception. It is the highest of the Green Mountains, and bears a fancied resemblance to the human face.

GLEN HOUSE.

See pages 216–217.

GLEN ELLIS FALLS,
Near Glen House.